"I haven't thanked you for rescuing me."

Vivian smiled at Billy, determined not to reveal any of her trepidation at his size and her vulnerability. "Thank you. You were an answer to a prayer."

He nodded solemnly. "You're welcome. I'm sure t'was God that led me there. No other reason I should be where I could hear you." He tipped his head toward the baby. "I guess, rightly speaking, it was this wee thing I heard."

Suddenly, the windows rattled as the door behind her opened. A cold breeze blasted across the room. She cuddled Joshua to her chest, protecting him from the icy invasion.

An older woman walked into the room, scrubbing her hands over her hair until it was a tangled mess. Vivian's jaw dropped. She suddenly realized who they were.

Mad Mrs. Black.

And her son, Big Billy.

Everyone was terrified of the pair. Rumors said they'd turned wild after being captives of Indians for years. But despite the talk, could he be anything but a good man if he acknowledged God's hand in rescuing her?

Books by Linda Ford

Love Inspired Historical

The Road to Love
The Journey Home
The Path to Her Heart
Dakota Child
The Cowboy's Baby
Dakota Cowboy

LINDA FORD

shares her life with her rancher husband, a grown son, a live-in client she provides care for, and a yappy parrot. She and her husband raised a family of fourteen children, ten adopted, providing her with plenty of opportunity to experience God's love and faithfulness. They had their share of adventures, as well. Taking twelve kids in a motor home on a three-thousand-mile road trip would be high on the list. They live in Alberta, Canada, close enough to the Rockies to admire them every day. She enjoys writing stories that reveal God's wondrous love through the lives of her characters.

Linda enjoys hearing from readers. Contact her at linda@lindaford.org or check out her website at www.lindaford.org, where you can also catch her blog, which often carries glimpses of both her writing activities and family life.

LINDA FORD
Dakota Child

Steeple
Hill®

Published by Steeple Hill Books™

STEEPLE HILL BOOKS

Steeple
Hill®

Recycling programs
for this product may
not exist in your area.

ISBN-13: 978-0-373-20273-7

Printed in U.S.A.

I have loved thee with an everlasting love;
therefore with loving kindness have I drawn thee.
—*Jeremiah* 31:3

To my grandson, Tyson.
I've watched you grow and mature
and my heart is filled with pride and joy.
I love you and pray God will bless you
all the days of your life.

Chapter One

Quinten, North Dakota, 1890

She was lost. The world had disappeared into swirling, biting snow. The rough ground beneath her feet convinced her she'd veered off the road. Her toe caught a lump and she staggered to keep her balance.

Nineteen-year-old Vivian Halliday's thoughts filled with a fury of denials. She couldn't be lost. No one would realize her predicament. No one would look for her. No one knew where she was. *Lord, God, help me.*

The same prayer she'd uttered so many times. Not for herself. She knew she didn't deserve it. There were times she hadn't listened to God or followed His voice as she ought. There were times she'd totally ignored Him and done her own thing. But she prayed for another and, lately, her prayer had grown more urgent. Today, however, her need was solid and desperate. The cold had already tightened her ribs to the point she could barely breathe, but thinking about how much she had to lose gave icy spears to the cold as it clawed into her lungs.

Snow coated her cheeks and iced her lashes. The wind tore at her cloak. She pulled the heavy woolen material tighter, then bent her head low and turned her back to the storm, letting it push her. It mattered not where she went. One direction was the same as another in this white wilderness.

"God, help me," she called, but the wind whipped her words into silence. She stumbled. Righted herself. Swayed.

A mewling sound came from inside her cloak.

The tiny cry filled her with fresh determination and she lifted her head and peered into the white nothingness.

She must escape this storm. She just had to keep moving and find shelter. Nothing must defeat her—not man, not beast, not beastly weather. *Lord, God, in You I trust. Save me.*

Snow blasted around her. Dizziness swept over her until she felt like she rode the circling wind. She could no longer tell up from down and melted into the cold, snow-shrouded ground.

The thin sound, from close to her heart, came again. All her pulses crashed against her skin like thunder. She would give her life to save the tiny life she sheltered.

She shook the basket cradled beneath the meager protection of the cape, trying unsuccessfully to still the protesting sound. Was her precious bundle suffering from the cold? She dare not look and allow even a hint of the cold to enter the shelter under her cape.

Suddenly, a huge shape darkened the snow to her left. She shrank back, her limbs brittle with fear. Was it a bear? A wandering, angry bull? She rocked harder. *Hush. Hush.*

"Someone there?" the massive shape bellowed.

Vivian sank back, trying to disappear into the snow. She crushed the basket closer and patted the sides.

The bulky figure swept trunk-sized arms about, searching for the source of the sound that wouldn't stop despite all Vivian's desperate measures. The cold bit at her throat. The wind howled louder. She prayed it would drown the sound coming from beneath her cape.

The creature—be it man or otherwise—encountered her shoulder with his great paw.

She stiffened. Perhaps he'd think her a bush and move on.

Fingers probed gently down her arm then up and across her back.

She held her breath. *Lord, God, save us.* She wanted to be left alone to find her way to town and safety. Instead, she was swept into strong arms, the cloak tucked around her, her face pressed into a broad shoulder. Then with great strides the huge creature plowed into the storm.

Protests formed but her lips refused to work, frozen with both cold and fear. One solitary thought remained in sharp focus—being captured by a wild man did not fit into her plans.

The wind held less bite. The cold's sting moderated. Must be the bulk of the man protecting her.

The last remnant of warm blood jolted through her veins. She would not find protection in the arms of a stranger. She struggled to escape.

"Settle down. I'll get you to a warm, safe place."

The thought of warmth enticed. But safety? She might be safer in the storm. She opened her mouth to protest but the cold grabbed her throat. She couldn't speak and her ineffectual efforts to escape allowed the snow to sneak under her cloak, robbing her of the bit of warmth his arms provided. She resisted for the space of another heartbeat, but the safety of his chest proved too alluring and she burrowed deeper into the bulky protection.

"That's better," he murmured, as he continued his hurried journey. His footsteps thudded hollowly as if his boots encountered wood, then he bent forward and took another step.

The wind ceased. A golden light washed over Vivian's eyelids. Loath to face reality, fearing it might be unkind, she kept her eyes shut.

Her rescuer shifted and lowered her into a chair.

"Let's see what you have here." His huge hands brushed her arm as he spread open her cape. Strong fingers began to unwrap her grip on the basket.

"No." She jerked her eyes open as alarm returned so fierce and overpowering that her heart thudded against her chest. She stared into a square face, half buried in a thick fur hat. Eyes as blue as a spring sky regarded her with what she could almost describe as amusement. His mouth tipped to one side in a wry expression. The man was huge, towering over her, blocking everything except bright flames from the fireplace at her side. For a moment, she ignored her fears and her need to protect all that was hers and darted a longing look at the promise of heat.

"I'll just have me a little look." He again sought to open the basket.

The cold tormenting Vivian's skin and bones balled up inside her heart and froze there. She clutched the basket more tightly to her chest and hunched her shoulders protectively as if she could defend herself against this giant. "Just let me sit here a minute until I'm warm," she choked out.

His eyes narrowed. His mouth drew into a thin line. "I ain't about to hurt you none." He waited.

Did he expect her to believe him? She darted a look at his mitt-sized fist on the handle of the basket. He could crush her with one hand. The damage he could do to a smaller body, an infant, was beyond imagination.

She shivered, and not from cold.

The mewling sound came again, louder, more demanding. Was everything all right? She ached to be able to check but instead clutched the basket closer and prayed he would leave her alone.

"Let's have a look," the giant said, and lifted her hand easily from the handle even though she squeezed as hard as she could.

She sprang forward, ready to defend. Realizing how futile her efforts would be, she frantically tried to think what she could do. Seemed the best she could hope for was that she could move faster than he. She tried to force her muscles to coil into readiness despite their numb coldness and found them stiffly uncooperative.

He put the basket on a stool before the fireplace. The warmth of the yellow-and-orange flames made her ache to hunker down and extend her hands. But she didn't dare move. Who knew what would trigger this man into action? And she wasn't about to hazard a guess as to what sort of action he might take. Instead she waited, alert and ready to protect what was hers.

He bent over and eagerly folded back the blanket to reveal the contents, then jumped back as if someone shot him. "It's a baby," he muttered. The look he fired her accused her of some sort of trickery. "I thought you had a cat."

His eagerness at thinking cat and his shock at seeing baby were such a marked contrast to what she expected, she almost laughed with relief. Fearing her amusement would spark anger in the man, she changed her mind before the feeling reached either her lips or her eyes.

He fixed her with a probing stare. "What you doing out in a storm with a baby?"

"I got lost." Did he really think she planned to be out with this precious infant? The man who gave her a ride toward Quinten, her hometown and destination, had dropped her off with an apology that he must take the other road, and assurances she was only a few miles from town and could easily walk the distance.

He obviously hadn't expected it to storm and if there'd been signs of its approach, she hadn't noticed. The storm caught her in the face as unexpectedly as if she'd fallen. In the driving wind she must have gotten turned around. Once the snow engulfed her, all that mattered was protecting the baby.

The man leaned forward and peered cautiously into the basket. "A boy or girl?" The huge man shifted his gaze to her, his eyes curious.

Vivian smiled. "A boy." The sweetest, fairest, most precious little boy in the whole world. She would never allow anyone to take him from her again. And she'd fight this giant of a man with everything at her disposal if she must.

"How old is he?"

"Almost two months." Seven weeks, four days and—at last reckoning of the time—six hours.

The baby's thin cry continued.

"I think he's hungry. Maybe you should feed him." The man nodded at her chest.

Vivian's cheeks thawed instantly. He expected her to nurse the baby. "There's a bottle in the basket." She'd have to find a source of milk as soon as possible. She stilled the panic twisting her heart. Where would she find milk in this place? She suddenly had a hundred different details to consider. She knew nothing about caring for a baby despite the few lessons Marie had given her. Marie had always been the one to gravitate toward the infants in the orphanage, while Vivian sought sanctuary in the kitchen. And when she'd been sent out to work for the Weimers, there had been no babies. How would she manage?

The man tossed his hat to one side. His dusty-yellow hair tangled in a mess of curls. Something stirred at the back of Vivian's mind. He seemed vaguely familiar. She tried to think where she'd seen him, but before she could figure it out he leaned over, scooped the baby from the basket and offered the bundle to Vivian.

She looked into a wrinkled and squalling face. Suddenly, an incredible ache filled her and she cradled her son to her chest, stilling a sob but unable to stop her eyes from growing moist. She might not know about caring for this little one but she knew about loving him and wanting him. The rest would follow.

"He got a proper name?"

She had not been allowed to name him legally but

had, in her thoughts, given him her father's name. "Joshua. After my father."

"Big name for such a little bitty thing."

"He'll grow—" She slid an amused glance at the big man. "Some."

He looked startled and then his eyes crinkled with understanding. "Ain't too many get to my size, but his name will suit, I 'spect."

Vivian smiled at the baby. "It suits him just fine." For some reason it did. "Can you hand me the bottle?"

He pulled it from the basket, hesitated. "You want I should warm it?"

"Oh, of course." She knew that. Just hadn't thought of it. Again, doubts grabbed at her resolve. Someone else should be caring for this tiny scrap of humanity. Someone who knew how to tend a baby. Remembering the seven weeks, four days and six hours when someone else did, she forced away her uncertainty. No one else should care for this baby but her. She would learn how just like every first-time mother did.

As the man moved to plop the bottle in the open kettle hanging over the flames, cats sprang from every corner of the room, meowing and clamoring around him.

"Now, you all just settle down. Ma will be in with your milk soon 'nough. This here is for that noisy fellow over there." He rubbed the heads of several of the animals.

Ma? The man was married. That boded well for

Vivian and Joshua. And they milked a cow. She relaxed fractionally and jiggled the crying baby as she waited for the man to take the bottle from the hot water, and let some of the contents drip into his mouth.

"Seems about right." He handed it to her.

She'd only fed the baby a couple of times before and always with the help and supervision of someone who knew how to do it with ease and comfort. Even on her ride today, the farmer's wife had begged to give him his bottle. She took a deep breath, prayed the baby would know more about what to do than she, and popped the nipple into the open mouth. The baby stopped crying and gagged.

Vivian jerked the bottle away and stilled her panic. What if she drowned the poor little thing? Maybe they were right in thinking she wasn't fit to raise him. Again she yanked her thoughts back from heading in that direction. She'd endured almost eight weeks of aching arms and a weeping heart. Never again would she go through that.

Praying she wouldn't harm him, she nudged the bottle into the baby's mouth again. He pushed at the nipple with his tongue, swallowed back a mouthful of milk, looked startled then settled into sucking.

She slowly let her lungs relax. This wasn't so bad.

She glanced about the room. The brick fireplace filled most of the wall to her right. A recessed area beside it held split logs. Braided rugs lay on the polished wood floor in front of the chair where she sat,

and before the wooden rocking chair facing her. On
the far side of the room was a kitchen table in rich
brown wood and the normal kitchen things—chairs,
stove, cupboards. A straw broom leaned in the corner
next to the stove, along with a bucketful of kindling.
At the corner opposite the fireplace a basket of raw
wool and some carders sat beside a low chair. To one
side, a quilt in muted grays and browns lay half rolled
on a frame. Two narrow windows revealed nothing but
white. The storm continued. How long would she be
stranded here waiting for it to end? Stuck with a man
who could easily harm them. But the room showed all
the signs of ordinary farm life. She almost breathed
scents of a happy, contented home and this squelched
her fears. Surely she and the baby would be safe even
with this huge man until such time as she could
complete her journey. All she had to do was be as quiet
and unobtrusive as possible. The chair she sat in had
stuffed arms and she let herself sink into the deep
cushions.

Joshua sucked at a leisurely pace as if he hadn't
been demanding food for the last half hour. Then he
stopped. She jiggled the bottle. He'd only taken half
an inch. Surely he needed more. Didn't he? She truly
had no idea.

"Little guy needs a burp, maybe."

Vivian nodded. Marie had told her that. She'd seen
it done. How hard could it be? Gingerly, she lifted the
baby to her shoulder and patted his tiny back. Warm

and cuddly, he made snuffling sounds against her neck and she smiled.

He let out a noisy burp and she laughed. Such a large sound from such a tiny body.

She resumed feeding him. The next time he stalled, she knew enough to burp him. This wasn't so hard after all, even with that big man watching her. She darted a glance at him. His gaze lingered on the baby with a look of amusement. She tried to place the twinge of recognition. Where had she seen him? She scoured her memory but came up empty.

Only a bit of milk remained in the bottle. Joshua curled in her arms, already asleep. So this is what they meant by sleeping like a baby. So peaceful, so relaxed and content. Her love for her son warmed and sweetened her insides.

She shifted, thinking to put Joshua back in the basket, but changed her mind. She liked the comfort of his little body, the way he settled against her as if welcoming her care.

"You got clean nappies?" the man asked.

Vivian kept her attention on the baby. Change wet pants? She could handle that. She wished she'd paid more attention to Marie's instructions but at the time she'd been far more concerned with making her escape before Matron or some of her helpers prevented it.

No doubt everything she needed was in the shopping basket, which served nicely for carrying baby supplies. Marie had prepared it for her saying no one who saw her would suspect the basket held a baby.

She pulled the basket closer. Yes, a wad of white nappies, a tiny blue sweater set and several white nighties lay in the bottom. She pulled out a nappy and looked from it to the baby. Where? How? Could she really do it?

The man pushed the stool closer. "You could lay him here."

"Thanks." She sucked in a deep breath and carefully transferred the baby. She unwrapped him from the bundle of blankets until he lay exposed in his nightie. His tiny fists curled against his chest. She rolled back the skirt to expose thin legs and amazingly small feet in blue booties. Her heart pushed up in her throat as a wave of tenderness washed through her. Her baby. Her son. So little. So perfect.

And wearing a dampish nappy fixed with big pins.

Undoing the pins posed no problem. Nor did removing the wet nappy. But what to do with it? She settled for dropping it on the floor. The clean nappy was folded to fit. Vivian did her best to fix it back in place the way the other had been. *There you go.* She resisted the urge to say the words aloud as she pulled Joshua's nightie down and wrapped him up again, quietly smug with her success. 'Course, she shouldn't take all the credit. God helps fools and children. He certainly had taken care of her this day. She could well be frozen to death—Joshua, too—if not for this man, who was no doubt guided by God's divine hand….

"I haven't thanked you for rescuing me." She smiled, determined not to reveal any of her trepidation at his size and her vulnerability. "Thank you. You were an answer to a prayer."

He nodded solemnly. "You're welcome. I'm sure 'twas God that led me there. No other reason I should be where I could hear you." He tipped his head toward the baby. "I guess rightly speaking, it was this wee thing I heard."

She met his eyes squarely. Despite his size, could he be anything but a good man if he acknowledged God's hand in rescuing her?

The windows rattled as the door behind her opened. A cold breeze, straight from the jaws of the storm, blasted across the room. She cuddled Joshua to her chest, protecting him from the icy invasion.

The man at her side, who had been hunkered down on a sturdy wooden stool, bolted to his feet. "Ma's back. Ma, Ma…"

But whatever he meant to say was drowned by an ear-splitting scream.

Vivian jerked to her feet and spun around.

A woman swaddled in a bulky woolen coat and hat faced her, a bucket of frothy milk in one hand. The woman put the pail on the floor, yanked her hat off and rubbed her pale hair into wild disarray, all the time making the sound of a cat with its tail slammed in the door.

Bony fingers of fear dug into Vivian's scalp. She tried to back up but ran into the stool she'd used a few minutes earlier for changing the baby. The fireplace blocked her retreat to her left; the big man blocked her right.

The screeching woman stopped to suck in air.

"Ma, I found them in the storm. I couldn't leave them to freeze."

The woman scrubbed her hands over her hair again until it was a cloud of faded blond tangles. "Nobody comes here. Nobody." Her voice shivered along Vivian's nerves.

Vivian's jaw dropped. Although she hadn't seen this woman or her son in eight years, she knew who they were.

Mad Mrs. Black.

And her son, Big Billy.

Everyone was terrified of the pair. Rumors said they turned wild after being captives of Indians for years. Vivian scrambled to remember what she knew or heard. But it was just before her own disaster. Seems she'd misplaced bits of her memory along with losing her parents and home. About all she knew was she couldn't have landed in a worse situation.

She clutched the baby to her chest and prayed to be able to save him from this savage pair.

Chapter Two

He saw the way she jolted. Knew she'd figured out who they were. Knew, too, what direction her thoughts took. He'd heard the comments often enough, seen hands raised to mouths to unsuccessfully hide a whisper. Everyone thought the Blacks were mad and dangerous. He'd long ago given up trying to prove otherwise, no longer cared what people thought so long as they left him and Ma alone. Though, if he could convince just one person it wasn't true, it would be the woman standing wide-eyed with fear not inches from his elbow.

But he didn't have time to deal with that right now. Ma was about to explode before his very eyes. She didn't handle strangers well, never let anyone in her house.

Ma choked off another screech, sent Vivian another fear-filled look, then glared at Billy. "Why'd you bring her?" She poked her mittened hand toward the woman as if she could drive her away. "Get out."

"Ma, it's okay. It's only until the storm lets up."

He couldn't remember a time when she didn't go from an ordinary housewife to this raving creature when anything upset her routine, though he guessed before she'd been captured by Indians, she'd been perfectly normal. However, he was too young at the time to remember.

Ma cranked around.

Sensing her intention, Billy strode for the door. Only the fact she struggled with the latch allowed him to get there before she opened it. He took her hands. "Ma, what are you doing?"

"Let me go." Her voice was thin and high-pitched.

"Ma, you can't go out. It's storming." He took her restless hands, guided her to the kitchen area and pulled out a chair. He tried to ease her down, persisting until she gave in and sat. As soon as he released her, she jerked the chair around so she gave her back to the woman.

Ma hadn't even glanced at the baby. Maybe if she did… For some unknown reason, he wanted Ma and Vivian to be friends. A little jeering finger jabbed inside his thoughts. In a mocking voice, it insisted Billy knew the reason. But Billy had grown very good at ignoring things he couldn't do anything about, and he shut out the voice.

"Ma, there's a tiny baby. You want to see him?"

For answer, she started to rock.

He took that for no. For himself, he could barely take his eyes off the little critter. He'd nursed every kind of baby animal—kittens, puppies, a fawn, several kinds of birds, the usual calves and colts. But he'd never seen a bitty-sized human. Tiny little fingers and toes, a kiss of a mouth, ears that folded like spring buds, legs no bigger than his little finger. New life was such a miracle of God's powerful love and creative power. But this replica of humanity took his breath away. Everything in perfect tiny detail. He knew a protectiveness stronger than he'd ever known before. He thought of the few minutes when he'd held Vivian in his arms, plowing through the storm toward home. He hadn't known it was her until he dropped her in the chair but he remembered the almost nothingness weight of her, the way she had fought so bravely and then the sweetness of her head pressed to the hollow of his shoulder as she huddled against the cold. He curled his fists. He was being fanciful and tried to remember how to push his thoughts beyond acknowledgment.

It took a few seconds for him to succeed, then he shifted his attention to Vivian. He liked the way she cradled the baby to her, though perhaps as much out of fear as any other reason. Everyone was afraid of the Blacks.

However, good or bad, she was stuck here until

the storm ended. Just as Ma was stuck with the un-invited pair.

"I guess you figured out who we are." Seeing her again made him wish for a heartbeat his life was different. Only half a heartbeat, really.

The woman nodded. "I remember you from school."

"Didn't know if you'd recall." He'd gone to school less than two weeks before he figured out he wasn't exactly welcome. He recalled only one person who had treated him kindly. He'd almost decided to continue to face his tormentors in order to see her—Vivian Halliday. Looks to be she was now other than Halliday. Married with a baby. With a practiced hand, he pushed aside any hint of regret. He only hoped she was happy.

"You're Billy Black."

"Huh." He was surprised she didn't call him Big Billy Black. It was the only way he'd ever heard his name said in town.

"You probably don't remember me. I was barely twelve last time I was in Quinten. Vivian Halliday."

She'd called herself Halliday. Perhaps an uncon-scious slip of the tongue.

"I remember." He'd recognized her the instant her eyelids snapped open and he looked into coffee-brown eyes revealing fear, and lots more besides. He saw flickers of the determination and gentleness he remem-bered from school. How often he'd thought of her and wondered how she fared.

He hadn't even realized she was gone at first, though he wondered that he never managed to glimpse her. 'Course, he avoided town as carefully as he avoided crossing paths with a skunk. Only necessity drove him to venture in by way of alleys.

It was Lucas, the man at the general store, who served him at the back door, who told him of the Halliday's misfortune.

"Mr. and Mrs. Halliday were among those who died in the flu epidemic. Their daughter went to an orphanage."

Remembering what happened to Vivian, Billy's fists still clenched. He would have given her a home. A curl of amusement lifted one corner of his mouth. Yeah, he could see anyone agreeing to that.

Best he face the situation head-on. "I guess you know what everyone else knows. That I'm too big to be trusted and Ma is crazy."

Vivian shifted her gaze from Ma to him. He saw the same compassion tucked beneath her fear that he'd seen eight years ago and had never been able to forget. Somewhere beyond the reach of his control, long-denied yearnings tossed rebellious heads reminding him of all the things he couldn't have—and somehow they all centered in this particular woman. He did his best to ignore the treacherous thoughts. She had always been out of reach and now even more so as a married woman. He had only one concern—keeping her safe until she could get back to her home.

As if aware no one watched her, Ma bolted to her feet and made a break for the door.

Billy didn't need to hurry to beat her to it. He leaned against the wooden barrier and crossed his arms over his chest. It about killed him to see her this way. What people didn't know was she didn't act crazy all the time. Only when something upset her bad, and nothing upset her like having a stranger close by. Couldn't get much closer than in her own house. She must be knotted up inside like an old hunk of neglected rope. He hated opposing her but he had to make sure Ma wouldn't hurt herself.

"Let me go." Ma's words were breathless as if forced from forgetful lungs.

"You ain't going into the storm."

Ma darted a glance out of the corner of her eye, indicating the stranger in their midst. "Can't stay here. You know what they say."

He knew. Had heard more'n he cared to. "Crazy Indian woman." "Unnatural giant." Neither was true. No one, not even he, knew what Ma had suffered in captivity but she had been a good and affectionate mother since her return. And Billy didn't figure he was that big. He'd met a couple of muleskinners even bigger.

"She's got to stay until the storm ends. She and the little one. They'd die outside."

Ma nodded. "I know. But I can't stay. I can't stay."

He led her back to the chair. "I'll make sure she

doesn't bother you." He waited until his mother settled before he threw a length of wood into the iron staples on either side of the door, effectively barring it. He knew from experience Ma couldn't lift the heavy piece out of place.

She keened like a woman bereft of her baby. The sound drove nails to Billy's heart. It was not like he had any choice. Vivian and her baby had to stay until the storm ended. And he had to keep Ma from running out into the cold.

He faced Vivian, her brown eyes wide in what he took for fear. The hood of her cloak fell back to reveal damp brown hair in a soft roll. The cloak slipped down her shoulders. From the little he could see, it appeared she wore a plain gray dress. She must have married a man of simple means. The idea caused him to swallow hard. She deserved to wear fine things like lace and velvet.

"Ma won't hurt you."

With a flick of her eyelids, without uttering a word, she effectively expressed her doubt.

"Your husband will be out looking for you." Would he have another stranger in their midst before night-fall? Ma would have a really hard time with another person stranded in her house, especially a man.

"I don't expect so." She shifted her eyes toward the fire, as if fascinated with the bright flames.

"But…" 'Twere none of his business, but if he had a wife and wee son he would not rest unless he was certain they were safe. Perhaps they'd argued and she wondered if her husband would let angry words keep him from action. But love quickly forgave. "He'll want to be sure you've found shelter—especially with the baby so small."

She shifted, darted a look at him. In the brief glimpse of her wide brown eyes, Billy saw something that set his mouth into a hard line. He'd seen fear. "Are you running from your husband? Afraid of him for some reason?" She need not fear a cruel man so long as Billy was around.

"No. Not at all." Her fingers moved restlessly against her son's blanket.

Billy wasn't much for beating around the bush. "Then what were you doing out in the storm when you should be safe in your home?"

She dragged her gaze toward him, shifted to study Ma's back, then back to stare at Billy.

Again he saw fear, accompanied by uncertainty. He tried to be indifferent to it. After all, she was another man's wife. Up to that man to protect and comfort her. But he wasn't here to provide it at the moment, and Billy took half a step toward her then caught himself. "He'll be worried over the little one." He held her gaze in an invisible grip, inviting the truth. Silently assuring her she was safe with him in every way.

"He doesn't know."

He heard the words but they made not a lick of

sense. "Doesn't know you're out, lost in the storm 'cept for God leading me to you?"

She worked her lips back and forth. Swallowed hard. "About the baby."

"Vivian, you ain't making a lick of sense." Had the cold affected her brain? "Of course your husband knows about the baby."

"I am not married." The whispered words seemed to escape against her will and as soon as she spoke them, she clamped her lips together. All expression disappeared from her face as if she'd wiped it away with a corner of the baby blanket. Though if he looked real hard he could see just a bit of something hurt and defensive, like the look in the eyes of the puppy he'd ripped from the hands of the man he found trying to shake it to death.

Knowing she expected some cruel word or gesture, he took care to reveal none of his shock, but, despite having lived with censure most of his twenty-two years, knowing she had a baby out of wedlock brought a sudden narrowing of his thoughts. Just as quickly, he let the criticism vanish. Everyone deserved a chance to prove himself. He'd offer this woman as much. On the heels of the realization she was unmarried came a flare of relief that he pointedly denied.

Her eyes narrowed as if she'd read something in his face—something he had meant to hide.

"He's mine." She splayed her hands over the baby. Her lips tightened.

Well, he never expected that. Had kind of thought she might see how relieved he was to know she wasn't married. Why, all of a sudden, was she insisting the baby was hers? He hadn't even considered otherwise, but her quick insistence and the defensive tone of her voice triggered misgivings in his mind. He carefully added up the things he noticed without heeding.

She didn't know enough to warm the milk.

Nor remember to change the wet pants without his reminder.

She was out in a storm. What could be bad enough to drive her out in this weather?

It all added up to suspicious. Was she in danger? If so, he would protect her. Or had she done something that would bring a posse down about the rafters? Even then, he would see she was treated fairly.

"I'm going to town to find Joshua's father. We'll make things right. You'll see."

He nodded, then turned to peer out the window. Snow plastered against the glass as if painted there by an unseen hand. His insides churned like he'd guzzled a gallon of sour milk. Why had this storm dumped her into his life, upsetting the peace his ma needed…triggering thoughts and desires he thought he'd successfully buried years ago?

He stilled the impatience in his heart knowing he could do nothing to change the weather except pray. He leaned against the wall, staring at the whitewashed window. *Lord, with one word You stopped the storm*

when You were on earth. Maybe You could see fit to say
a word or two today to stop this storm.

As soon as he could see to find his way, he'd take
Vivian and her baby to town. Before Ma came apart at
the seams. Aware of a faint call from some distant part
of his heart, he added, before his carefully constrained
life exploded out of control.

In the meantime, they needed shelter.

And the cats clamored to be fed. He rescued the
bucket from the floor where Ma abandoned it and
poured the milk through the clean cloth saved for that
purpose. He filled the half-dozen pans under the table
and the cats happily lapped at their dinner. He set jugs
of strained milk to cool. Good thing Ma insisted on
keeping the cow producing. Otherwise, how would
they feed the baby?

Funny, Vivian didn't nurse her baby. He mentally
added it to the list of things causing suspicion.

Vivian sank into the rocking chair where she could
keep her gaze on Ma's back. The air quivered with
tension from both women.

Billy stood at the cupboard, wondering how one en-
tertained a pretty, young guest. He could think of
nothing to talk about.

Cat and Fluffy crawled into Ma's lap and she
stroked them. Maybe that would calm her.

Billy eased back to the fireplace and hunkered down
on the stool he'd built specially for his weight. His
insides settled into claylike heaviness at the way Viv-

ian's arms tightened, and how she blinked as if startled. She might be kind but she still feared him.

"Got to be hard—on your own with a new baby."

She chuckled softly. He liked the sound of her amusement—soft and calming, reminding him of the wind through the top branches of the trees along the creek.

"Much harder than I dreamed." She ducked her head but not before he saw a flash of stubbornness.

He allowed a one-cornered smile to tip his mouth. He admired a person with lots of grit when it came to facing life's challenges. And he suspected Vivian had more than her share of difficulties tossed her way and yet she'd come back to Quinten as if to defy those circumstances. His smile fled, replaced with wariness that tightened his mouth. A stubborn woman could mean trouble for him and Ma. And no, he wouldn't welcome a bit of trouble for the enjoyment of some time spent with Miss Vivian.

The wind howled around the house, rattled the windows and sent shafts of cold across the floor. He didn't need to stir himself to know the storm worsened rather than let up. The room seemed overcrowded with Vivian and the baby in one corner, and Ma shivering in the other, and he went to the window and stared out. He longed to be able to trot out to the barn and check on the animals. But he didn't dare leave Ma alone.

Vivian's kindness had been so easily given when they were both at school. Truth was, he placed her on kind of a pedestal. Yet every instinct in him said she was going to turn his life inside out and upside down if he wasn't careful.

If only the storm would end.

Lord, why have You put me in this situation?

Was God expecting him to see no harm came to that little baby?

It was the only thing that made sense.

As if to confirm his thinking, the baby started to cry.

Ma let out an echoing protest and covered her ears. "Don't like baby crying."

Billy sighed. Life would not settle back to normal as long as this woman and the little one remained. He gave one more imploring look at the window, sent up one more imploring prayer for the storm to stop, then turned to face the room.

Ma rocked Cat and Vivian rocked the baby as it continued to wail.

Billy looked from one to the other. Seemed they both wore similar frantic expressions, each one scared and upset by the other.

Vivian pressed the baby against her neck and rocked harder and harder as the cries grew louder and louder.

Billy scrubbed his fist across his chin. Oh, for the peace of the outdoors.

"What's wrong with the little guy?"

Vivian shook her head. "I don't know. I suppose I could try feeding him again." She reached into the basket for the bottle.

That was another thing. The basket looked like something a woman would carry shopping in. Or store sewing materials. Not hardly big enough for the little critter. Was a wonder it hadn't suffocated. He squeezed at his thoughts, not wanting to shed one whiff of criticism on Vivian but it seemed she was running. From what? Was she in danger? His insides pushed at his bones. No one would hurt her while he was around.

Vivian found the bottle and examined its contents— an inch of old milk. She tipped the baby into the crook of her arm and hesitated.

Surely, she wouldn't give the baby that. When he saw she intended to do so, Billy reached for the bottle. "I'll get some fresh milk." He scrubbed the bottle in hot water before filling it. While it warmed, he studied Vivian.

She must have felt his eyes on her for she gave him a hard look. "What?"

"Nothing." He handed her the bottle. "Except, how come you know nothing about caring for a baby?"

She turned her attention to the infant. "Haven't had much experience. Have I, Joshua?"

"You said he's almost two months old." He let his words convey his doubt.

She didn't answer as she tried to persuade the little guy to take the bottle. But the baby screamed and gagged. "Come on, Joshua. Eat something. You'll feel better." She struggled to no avail. "Please, take the bottle." Her voice grew sharp, edged with desperation.

Ma rocked harder and moaned. Cat decided he'd had enough and scrambled from Ma's arms. Ma tried to grab the cat but it meant uncovering her ears and she quickly returned her hands to the sides of her head.

"Ma, pick up Fluffy. He'll let you hold him."

When Ma made no effort to do so, Billy strode over and scooped the cat into her lap. Ma shot him an accusing look as she wrapped the cat into her arms and returned her hands to her ears. At the sight of tears washing her face, Billy closed his eyes and prayed for patience and wisdom. The weather better change real quick before things went downhill any further.

The baby's protests turned to screaming. Milk ran down his cheeks and pooled in the folds of his neck.

Billy stated the obvious. "I guess he ain't hungry."

Vivian set the bottle aside, wiped the squalling face, and cleaned the baby's neck. The screaming continued, assaulting Billy's eardrums.

Fluffy squirmed in Ma's tight grasp. Tom and Tiger edged toward the sound, ears tipped in curiosity. The rest of the cats shrank back under the stove.

"Can't you make him stop?" Billy demanded.

"I would, if I knew what to do." She looked annoyed and frustrated at the same time.

"Why don't you know?" He waited as she scowled at him. "He ain't yours, is he?"

She snorted. "You wanting him? Right now, you could have him. Real cheap. Free, in fact."

Billy blinked. His mouth pulled down at the corners. "You can't give a baby away just because he's crying."

"No?" She pushed to her feet, took three steps and thrust the squalling bundle into Billy's arms. "You make him stop." She dropped back to the chair as if exhausted.

Billy couldn't move. He'd never felt anything like this little bitty human. He had to remind himself to breathe.

The baby weighed next to nothing, yet had the lungs of a cattle drover. The little bundle of noise drew in a breath, pulling his mouth into a pout.

The poor thing.

Billy lifted the baby to his chest and patted gently. The wails continued. Billy walked toward the door, turned and walked back. Were the screams less intense? He hummed the tune, "Fairest Lord Jesus, ruler of all nature."

The baby snuffled a bit, then grew quiet.

Billy let the sweetness of success, the incredible pleasure of holding this baby, fill his thoughts.

Ma stopped moaning, stopped rocking.

He kept humming, fearing the baby would begin his caterwauling again if he quit. He sank to the chair across from Vivian and continued the song.

Vivian sighed and tipped her head back.

Convinced there was something not right about this whole situation—a woman who admitted she wasn't married and obviously knew little about caring for the infant she claimed was hers—he tried to figure out a way to get the truth from her. But she could answer questions any way she chose. Truth or lie.

"You hiding from someone?" He kept his voice the same timbre as his hum, relieved the baby didn't protest and Ma seemed content murmuring comforting noises to Fluffy. A fragile peace settled about his taut nerves.

Vivian studied him intently.

He thought for a moment she intended to ignore his question.

"What concern is that of yours?"

The baby whimpered and Billy hummed for a few minutes before he answered. "I think it's my concern if someone is looking for a missing baby. Last thing I need is trouble with the law."

She gave a tight smile. "It seems to me you can handle most any trouble."

"You mean my size."

"I think it would be a good deterrent to any nosy parkers."

"I ain't talking about snoops. I'm meaning angry citizens or lawmen. I make a mighty big target for a bullet."

Again that look of defiance. "I'm not planning to stay." She glanced at Ma and gave the barest shiver.

Billy guessed she wasn't aware of it any more than she realized the fear in her eyes.

Tom and Tiger, the most curious of his cats, jumped

to his lap and nosed around the baby, sniffing and meowing. Tom, the more aggressive one, laid his ears back as if to say he didn't approve of sharing his space with this strange creature. "Tom, you be nice." Tom meowed innocently then edged under Billy's arm, making Billy chuckle. "You always got to be first, don't you?"

He felt a little foolish talking to his cats in front of this woman, and shut up.

"I'll be gone as soon as the storm lets up," Vivian assured him.

"It shows no sign of doing that." And suppertime approached. His stomach began squeezing his backbone. He didn't care to miss a meal. Nor delay it even a few minutes, but Ma didn't look about to make anything.

Vivian was a guest. She could hardly be called on to prepare food. Besides, she might expect him to eat like she did. In which case he'd leave the table as hungry as he was now.

That left him—with a sleeping infant in his arms. He shifted the tiny bundle and handed it back to Vivian.

The baby protested at the change of arms but didn't waken.

"I'll make us something to eat." He hated cooking. Seemed to take forever to prepare enough food to satisfy his appetite.

They had a good supply of venison; potatoes and turnips from the garden; eggs, milk, cheese and a storeroom with beans, flour and cornmeal. His mouth watered at the thought of fresh-from-the-oven corn bread drowned in molasses, but that took too long.

He pulled out three big fry pans and dropped a dollop of bacon drippings into each. As soon as it sizzled, he put venison chops in one pan and browned them. He cut leftover potatoes into the second and broke two dozen eggs into the third pan. He sliced a roll of Ma's bread and wished for some fresh green vegetables, but garden season was a long way off.

"It's ready. Come and get it." He filled a plate for Ma, filled another with an equal amount for Vivian and set them on the table. The rest he scooped to a platter for himself.

When Vivian rose, Ma jerked to her feet. "Don't come any closer."

Vivian stopped so fast she teetered.

Billy stared from one woman to the other, feeling as if he were caught in the middle of two storms, not knowing which one would intensify first, nor what damage each would inflict.

"Ma, we got to feed the woman. It's uncharitable not to."

"I'll leave," Ma said, and before Billy could think what she meant to do, she dropped Fluffy to the floor, grabbed her plate and retreated past the stove into the doorless pantry. She pressed into the farthest corner, out of sight.

"Ma."

"I'll eat here," she mumbled.

"I can eat here," Vivian said at the same time.

Billy wanted nothing more than to sit down and fill the hollowness some people called hunger. Instead, he had these two people—three, if you counted the baby—to contend with.

And a storm in his head as violent as the one raging outdoors.

Chapter Three

A shiver raced across Vivian's shoulders and reached down her throat to grab her heart in a cruel grip. She was hungry, yet she hesitated. Mrs. Black scared every last bit of courage from her heart.

"Ma won't be changing her mind. You might as well pull up to the table."

Vivian ducked her head to hide the sudden sting of tears. She longed to be safe. Until this morning, she had always chosen the easy route, doing what was expected of her. Her fear switched to anger. Look where that had landed her.

"I'm getting mighty hungry and when I'm hungry I get cranky." Billy sounded as if he'd already crossed the line into that state.

Realizing her precarious position, Vivian jerked as if lassoed unexpectedly from behind. She did not want to see Billy upset in any way. She remembered him from school. How he'd stood with fists curled as the boys taunted him. She'd wondered how they had the nerve to test Billy's mettle. Even back then he was big enough to do serious harm to several of them before they could stop him by the sheer weight of their numbers. As she'd watched, her heart tight with distress at their taunts, tears raced to her eyes. Then Billy looked directly at her. She'd seen the pain in his gaze and knew how much this tormenting hurt him. Then his anger exploded. Only he didn't turn on the boys responsible. He started pounding on the walls of the barn on the school property. She'd almost been ill at how he'd thrust his fists again and again into the unyielding wood until his knuckles were torn and bleeding.

She did not want to trigger such a violent reaction because of something she did or failed to do, so she slowly made her way to the table hoping he would think her shivers came from moving away from the fireplace.

To think she'd handed the baby to Big Billy. Certainly, his crying made her feel helpless and frustrated, but as soon as she shoved the bundle into his hands she knew she'd made a mistake. Billy had only to curl his big fists to squeeze the life out of the infant.

She'd held her breath, praying he would choose not to. God mercifully answered her prayers. The big man cradled the baby gently and the little bit of squalling intractability settled down.

Suddenly, her fears subsided and her heart calmed. Somehow, and she couldn't explain it, she knew Billy would not harm a living soul. Perhaps it was seeing how gentle he was with the numerous cats, or watching his patient concern over his mother or realizing that even in his anger almost eight years ago, he had not turned against those responsible.

She straightened her shoulders, shifted the baby and walked to the table. There were three chairs. She avoided the one vacated by his mother.

Billy waited until she sat, the baby cradled in her left arm. "I'll pray for the food."

Startled by his announcement, expecting him to care little about godly things, she darted a look at him, caught him watching her and quickly bowed her head.

"I ain't a bad man," he muttered.

She wanted to tell him she didn't think so, but when she stole another glance he had closed his eyes. Just as well. She wasn't sure what she thought of this big man. She, too, bowed her head.

"Lord, some have hunger, but no meat; some have meat, but no hunger; I have both. God be praised! Amen."

Vivian coughed to hide her sudden desire to laugh. She kept her head down, glad of the need to concentrate on her meal. She doubted Big Billy would share her amusement at the grace he'd chosen.

In the pantry, his mother mumbled something unintelligible but clearly was annoyed.

How did Billy live with this day in and day out? It was enough to drive even the strongest man to lunacy.

Anger gnawed at her throat. It wasn't her fault she was stuck with a crazy woman and a reluctant man. She had a clear-cut destination and a task to take care of. Only the storm had diverted her. *Lord, God, keep me safe, help me make it to town and enable me to accomplish my purpose.*

She ate slowly as she considered her situation and what she could do. Nothing for now. Except pray. She wished she hadn't told him the truth about being unmarried. It always made her feel dirty and stupid. She should have never listened to Wayne's promises. But if Billy felt the usual disgust at evidence of a woman with loose morals, to his credit he had hidden it.

Billy ate as if he'd never get another chance. He'd taken the platter she thought for serving food, and consumed the stack of potatoes, four venison steaks and well over a dozen eggs, used four thick slices of bread to clean his plate, then sat back with a huge sigh.

Aware she'd been staring these last five minutes, Vivian ducked her head but not before Billy noticed her interest.

"It takes a lot to fuel me."

She didn't say anything.

"Tea," his mother called.

"Coming, Ma." He tossed a handful of tea leaves into a big brown china teapot, poured in hot water and let it steep. "She's not always like this," Billy said. "Only when there's strangers about."

He was blaming Vivian, which wasn't fair. It wasn't her fault. As if aware of her upset thoughts, the tiny boy stiffened and whimpered. Her anger vanished and she murmured soft noises to the baby. "I'm sorry, son. I love you and will get you the sort of home you deserve."

Billy took a cup of tea to his mother. Vivian heard the woman mumbling her complaint, and Billy's deep voice responding, trying to reassure her. Somehow, despite his size and the timbre of his voice, he had the power to calm his mother. It seemed to work for the baby, too.

On his return, Billy offered Vivian tea.

"Thanks." Maybe it would soothe her nerves, growing tighter with each passing moment. In fact, if she listened carefully, she could hear them humming like frost-tight wires. She wanted only to get to Quinten. She hadn't been back since being whisked away to the orphanage seven years ago. She could hardly wait to start over as an adult, a mother and according to her plan, the wife of an upstanding citizen.

A cat rubbed against her leg, startling her. She gasped.

Billy studied her. "You scared of cats?"

"No. I just never had one rub against me while I sat at a table."

"You never had a pet cat?"

"No." Mother had considered cats dirty. The orphanage didn't allow pets. And the Weimers had cats only in the mill—wild, mangy things you couldn't get close to. Or want to.

"Then I guess you might find it unusual to have so many."

"How many are there?" She'd tried to count.

"Eight in the house. More in the barn."

"I'm guessing you don't have trouble with mice."

He chuckled. "Would have to be the bravest mouse in the world to hang around here."

His easy humor caught her off guard but before she had time to analyze her response, the baby lifted his voice in a demanding wail. She had no idea what he wanted this time. Who knew a baby could be so challenging? She had to figure out what to do with him. Billy already expressed suspicion because of her lack of knowledge in caring for an infant. She wished she could assure him there would be no lawmen after her, but despite the paper in her pocket and Marie's assurances…

She balanced the baby in one arm, retrieved the abandoned bottle from near the fireplace and prepared it as she'd seen Billy do. She persuaded Joshua to take the bottle. He sucked eagerly. She burped him when it seemed appropriate, and changed his nappy realizing she would soon have to wash the soiled ones or risk running out of clean ones.

Billy stayed at the window looking into the emptiness or alternately watching Joshua. Then he caught her gaze.

She blinked before the compassion in his look, wondering at its source.

"I heard about your ma and pa. I'm sorry."

"What did you hear?"

"Them dying and leaving you alone. How you got sent to an orphanage. Must have been real tough."

Sympathy from this unlikely source unlocked a hidden store of pain that escaped in a rush of words. "You can't begin to imagine. I lost everything. My family, my home and security. I went from being a loved and cherished only child to being nobody." She struggled to contain her emotions. She'd felt lost and alone, not just on that dreadful day, but every day following. She knew if she ever let the full force of her feelings escape they would turn into a flood of furious proportions. She sucked in air, pushing down the words, the feelings, the anger and pain.

She'd learned to deny her feelings and accept her fate. Perhaps too well.

Until Joshua.

His birth seemed to have planted a strength in her. Granted, it took almost two months for it to grow enough for her to act, but she was here now—evidence it had reached its potential.

"You are valued and loved by God. Your circumstances don't change that."

She met his steady blue gaze, let her thoughts follow

his words. "I know that." Her faith was part of who she was, part of what her parents left her, though people would have cause to wonder considering her present circumstance—a baby but no husband.

"You can trust God when you can't trust anyone else."

She couldn't break away from his look, guessed his words conveyed far more than she knew. "It's been tough for you, too." As soon as the whispered words were out, she wished she could pull them back. She didn't want to remind him of the cruelty of people; didn't know how he'd react.

Billy's expression went blank, almost stupid. "If you mean how people treat us, it don't matter to me. Ma and I don't need anyone else." He pushed to his feet. "I'm gonna clean up."

"I'll help." One thing she'd learned, you better make yourself useful or no one would bother with you. And despite her wishes to be somewhere else, she needed to stay here until the storm ended.

Joshua sucked his bottom lip as she laid him on his side in the stuffed chair. She touched his silky cheek. So beautiful. So sweet. So much responsibility but she would soon have help in raising him. As soon as she reached Quinten and contacted Wayne. One look at this beautiful child they had created together and marriage would be the first thing he'd want so they could give Joshua a loving home, and the benefit of Wayne's name.

She turned to help clean the table. Mrs. Black came to the doorway of the pantry, saw Vivian, covered her face and moaned.

Vivian halted. She didn't want to upset this woman any further. Slowly, she backed away. Mrs. Black did the same until she was out of sight.

"Just leave her be," Billy said, his tone mild, but she didn't make the mistake of thinking it carried no warning.

She wanted to protest. She'd done nothing to bother the woman except reluctantly find shelter under her roof, but that was obviously more than enough. She grabbed a drying towel from behind the stove. Billy had already washed several dishes and she dried them. They worked in silence.

One thought consumed her.

Would she have to stay here for the night? If so, she faced long hours of forcing her eyes to remain open. Mrs. Black's threatening looks made her afraid of what would happen if she slept.

"Looks like you're stuck here."

Billy's words confirmed her worst fears, gave them body and strength.

From the pantry, his ma screeched.

The sound gave Vivian's fears flesh and blood.

She polished a plate. She needed to count her blessings as Mother had taught her. She was in out of the storm where she would have surely frozen to death. The baby was safe and, best of all, they were together.

"I think it's dry."

Billy's slow words made Vivian realize how long she'd been wiping the plate and she handed it to him to put away.

"You'll be safe here. As safe as in your own home."

Vivian had learned the hard way you weren't safe even in your own home. Yet his words—or perhaps his tone—eased some of her tension.

They finished the dishes without further conversation.

"Ma," Billy called. "Come out now. You can sit by the fire and card wool."

"Noooooo."

The sound sent shivers up Vivian's spine and she again promised herself she would stay awake all night. Perhaps with a poker at her side.

"You'll be getting cold."

"Bring me my coat."

"No, Ma. You can't stay there." He went to the pantry. Ignoring a moaning protest, he slowly pulled his mother from the room, his big hands enclosing her smaller ones.

Vivian hung back, half hidden beside the warm kitchen stove.

Billy edged his ma toward the wooden rocker and waited until she bent her knees and dropped to its seat. He aimed his bulk toward the stuffed chair, saw the baby at the same time as Vivian cried out. Her heart rattled against her chest at the close call.

Mrs. Black moaned and tried to regain her feet but Billy planted a hand on her shoulder and waited for her to settle back, then he scooped up the baby and handed him to Vivian.

Something cold and itchy washed down her back as she cuddled the sleeping bundle, and edged to a wooden kitchen chair and sat so she could see the pair. It looked to be a long, fright-filled night ahead.

Billy pulled a big Bible from the mantel and opened it. In slow, measured tones he read the Twenty-third Psalm.

Mrs. Black rocked, never once taking her eyes from his face, her expression desperate as if clinging to her last shred of sanity by focusing on Billy's voice, or perhaps the words of scripture.

It was not a comforting thought.

Billy finished and replaced the Bible on the shelf.

"I like that psalm," Mrs. Black said.

"It's a good one, for sure." Billy threw more wood on the fire and glanced toward the stove where Vivian sat.

She knew he wanted to stoke the fire, sensed he hesitated to move for fear of bringing an end to his mother's calm. Vivian didn't offer to help, nor move to do so for the same reason. She tried to stifle a yawn. The long day and the time spent afraid and freezing in the storm had sapped her energy. Her head drooped. She snapped to attention. There'd be no sleep tonight.

"Ma, why don't you go to bed?"

Mrs. Black scrubbed at her hair, tangling it even worse. "I can't sleep with—" She tilted her head toward Vivian.

The way it made Vivian feel unwelcome was as familiar as it was despised. She pulled Joshua closer. She'd give him what she'd lost—a home. A place of belonging and acceptance.

She tried to picture the house where they would live but having never been inside as far as she could remember, she had to make up the details. However, she could picture the face of Joshua's father and she recalled every word he'd spoken to her. She should have taken them with a grain of caution but despite her many regrets at her foolishness, Joshua wasn't one of them. *My precious baby.*

As soon as the storm ended, she would head to town and her plan.

Billy's voice interrupted her thoughts. "Ma, you go to your bed and I'll make sure you're safe." Mother and son regarded each other for a long, tense moment, then Mrs. Black nodded.

"I'll not sleep."

"Nor I," Billy said.

Vivian silently echoed the words. Little Joshua was the only one inclined to sleep in this household tonight.

Mrs. Black disappeared into a doorway next to the pantry. She firmly closed the door even though they all knew it would also shut out the heat.

"You're welcome to take my bed," Billy said.

Dakota Child

Vivian shook her head hard. "Thanks, but I'll just wait for the storm to end." She again tried to count her blessings—safety, a chance to start over and the determination to work hard to achieve her goal.

Her head drooped again. She jerked upright. What if she dropped Joshua?

"Best move closer to the fire," Billy said. "The kitchen stove is getting cold."

Her feet grew icy and her arm ached from holding the baby. She studied the warm glow of the fire and considered what it meant to move closer.

Billy sighed, lumbered out of the big chair and pushed it several feet from the rocker. "That make you feel safer?"

Heat raced up her neck and settled in her cheeks as if she stood too close to the flames. She'd been rude. She normally didn't shun anyone, but his size, his mother's mental state… Well, who could blame her for her anxiety?

She crossed the room and settled in the chair, shifting Joshua to her chest to ease the strain on her arm, then faced Billy squarely. "I didn't mean anything."

His eyes were flashes of blue ice. His gaze looked through her, past her as if she wasn't there. It wasn't an unfamiliar feeling, nor a welcome one. She was done with being invisible, though perhaps this was not a wise time to inform the world, especially when the world consisted solely of Big Billy Black and his mad mother.

Suddenly, his look connected with hers so intently surprise raced through her. Then he gave an unexpectedly gentle smile.

She floundered for a solid thought.

"Know you didn't mean anything."

Her eyes widened of their own accord. She seemed unable to break from his look that went past her fear and through her emptiness to a spot deep inside that warmed and quivered like flower petals opening to the sun. When was the last time someone looked at her so, as if she mattered solely because she was a person? Not, she knew, since her parents died. Oh, sure, there'd been exceptions—Marie and Joshua's father—but they were few and far between and in the latter case, short-lived. But why it should be Billy resurrecting that feeling of being valued made no sense. Any more than his soft assurances that he knew she meant no harm by her statement. "How could you know that?"

His smile deepened. His gaze warmed even more. "Because I remember you in school." He paused, and shifted his gaze to the fire and then back to her.

She saw something new in his eyes—was it longing? She couldn't say for certain, but the look brought a flood of sadness to her heart.

He nodded slightly. "I remember your kindness."

"My kindness?" She managed to stammer out the words. "I don't remember doing anything."

"I know." His words were soft, like a whispered

benediction. "Your kindness comes natural. It's a part of you."

"It is?" Her mouth rounded with disbelief. No one ever said anything so approving before and it made her feel— She struggled to identify this sensation of…of being really seen. Valued. And from a source she least expected. "What did I do?"

"You offered me a cookie."

"I did?" She had no memory of the event. "Did you take it?"

He chuckled, a deep-throated rumble resounding in his chest and bringing a smile to her lips. "I have never been one to refuse food."

She laughed. "Maybe I knew it even back then."

"You were the only one who was nice to me. You didn't seem afraid of my size."

They studied each other. She didn't know what his watchful gaze wanted. What she saw was a big, kind man trying his best to hide his hurt at being treated poorly. He wore a faded blue shirt that brought out the color in his eyes. His fawn-colored trousers were sprinkled with cat hair in variegated colors. He wore heavy socks knit in raw wool and lounged in the chair as if life held nothing but joy for him.

She knew otherwise. And she knew more. This man would never harm her. In fact, she would trust him to protect her if the need arose. The thought comforted. "I'm not afraid of you."

Hope raced across his expression and disappeared so quickly she almost missed it.

Satisfaction smoothed away her tension. She'd brought a bit of well-deserved well-being to this man.

He stared into the flames, the reflection of the fire's glow softening his face.

She remembered how she'd sheltered against his shoulder as he carried her from the storm. It reinforced her feeling he was the sort of man one could count on. If not for his ma, this would be a safe and sheltering place. She stopped her thoughts right there and stared into the flames. She was letting the warmth of the fire and the isolating roar of the wind divert her thoughts from her goal. She must find Joshua's father. Together, they would build a happy home even though she didn't know if she felt anything toward the man except regret at what they'd done, and gratitude for her son.

She stole a glance out of the corner of her eye, saw that Billy watched the baby as he stroked a lap full of cats. Other cats curled around his feet. The noise of so many purrs made her laugh.

He smiled crookedly. "I spoil them."

"They're your friends." There was something oddly appealing about such a big man enjoying pets.

His eyes narrowed. "Better than friends. They don't judge or condemn."

She understood his reluctance to trust people. She shared the lesson. But through it all, she had Marie, a special friend whose support sustained her. "Not every-one is the same. I had a friend in the orphanage who always helped me." Even if Marie got herself into all sorts of awkward situations, she never failed to help Vivian when she needed it.

Joshua stiffened in her arms and wailed.

Billy bolted to his feet with surprising agility. "I'll get the bottle."

Joshua took the bottle readily and Vivian settled back, rocking gently. A person could get used to this so long as they knew what to do.

Billy snored softly.

Vivian smiled. So much for not going to sleep. She rested her head on the back of the rocker and closed her eyes. The storm still raged outside as questions raced around inside her head.

Who was she? Vivian Halliday. But who was that? She didn't know. She'd lost all sense of who she was when her life had been stolen from her. Or had she let people take it from her degree by degree?

It no longer mattered because from now on, her every thought and decision would be on Joshua's behalf and for his good.

She smiled, her eyes still closed.

True, taking the baby from the orphanage wasn't entirely an unselfish act. Yes, she wanted her baby to have more than a foundling home could offer, or even an adoption. But it had been to quench the hunger of her own heart that had spurred her to go against everything she'd been told to do.

Yes, Joshua's birth had given her a strength that had before been foreign to her.

Chapter Four

A sharp sound pierced Billy's sleep and he jerked awake. When he realized he slept in the big chair, he moaned. He'd promised Ma to stay awake and guard her. Not that he figured Vivian or the baby meant to harm them.

He scrubbed the sleep from his eyes. The rocking chair was empty. He bolted to his feet. Where had they gone?

The high-pitched sound echoed inside his brain. He shook his head to clear away the sleep fog. Vivian stood near the window now blackened by darkness and streaked with bits of snow. She jostled the baby— the source of such shattering noise. Her eyes were wide with distress.

"I'm sorry he woke you but I can't get him to stop crying."

"Maybe he's hungry."

"I tried feeding him."

"Wet pants?"

"No."

"Tummy ache?"

Her mouth dropped open. "Now, how would I know?"

He chuckled. "I guess he's telling you the best way he can. He often have tummy aches?"

She turned her attention back to the baby but not before he caught what he guessed was a hint of surprise and confusion.

There was something odd about Vivian and this baby. Her affection and protective attitude were real enough, yet her inexperience seemed out of place.

She sighed.

He gave her a hard look now that the cobwebs had cleared from his mind. She looked as if she'd been wrung out and hung in a stiff wind to dry. "The little one been fussing long?"

"I've tried to keep him quiet so he wouldn't wake you or—" She tipped her head toward Ma's door. "But he simply won't settle down."

As if to prove her words correct, the baby arched his back and screamed louder.

Ma snorted.

Billy held his breath waiting to see if Ma would set up her own protesting racket. When he heard soft snores, he eased air out of his lungs. "Give him to me."

Vivian didn't argue. Didn't even protest. In fact,

she seemed as eager as a Dakota spring was reluctant to rid herself of the squalling infant.

He cradled the baby to his chest and hummed as he walked the floor. The baby cried at first and then slowly quieted. Billy continued to walk because every time he stopped, the baby stiffened and whimpered.

Vivian curled up in the stuffed chair before the warm fire and in minutes fell asleep.

Billy walked until he was sure a pathway across the floor marked his journey. He hummed until he grew both hoarse and amazed a little critter could outlast the reserves of a huge adult. When the infant finally seemed relaxed, Billy dropped wearily to the rocker, sighing relief when the baby didn't fuss.

He closed his eyes, let his head fall back and listened. The wind had moderated. He figured the storm would end with first light and unless the drifts were impassable, he'd have Vivian and the baby in town by noon.

Then he and Ma could return to normal—the quiet calm of Ma working about the house, milking her cow, tending the chickens; his satisfaction in caring for all his animals and walking alone across the prairie. That was his life.

He closed his eyes, gritted his teeth and denied a desire for more. No point in wishing for stars when he lived in plain old farm dirt. His world was what it was.

He was unreasonably glad when Joshua started to

fuss again and he could turn his thoughts to something else.

Vivian barely stirred so Billy fed the baby, smiling as the tiny fist curled around Billy's little finger. He rubbed Joshua's cheek, amazed at the smoothness of his skin, like a polished rock warm in the sun.

Vivian had washed out the nappies and hung them to dry. Billy wondered how to fold one to fit the baby. Had no idea. Best he wait and let Vivian do it.

He and the baby sat warm and content in front of the fire. He watched the flames twist and turn, and wondered about Vivian. Why had God seen fit to dump her on his doorstep? If she needed help, he would willingly provide it. He rested his face against Joshua's warm head. It pleased him to see Vivian and the baby together. God knew a child needed and deserved the love of his mother.

Billy snorted in surprise at the direction of his thoughts. This wasn't about what happened to him. It was about protecting Vivian and the baby until the storm ended. Then they'd be gone. Some unfamiliar portion of his brain wondered what it would be like if he could keep them.

The room lightened. The frost-covered window turned gray.

The baby stretched. Billy turned the little bundle into his palms and stared into wide eyes as blue as the deep pond of water where the best fish hid. Joshua puckered his lips in an expression as wise and knowing as an ancient sage. It was so serious and comical at the same time, Billy chuckled. "Never seen anyone like me before, have you?"

As the baby blinked solemnly, Vivian woke with a gasp. "I didn't mean to sleep."

"That's what most people do at night."

She snorted. "If they're safe in their own bed."

"You're just as safe." He understood people's fears of Ma's crazy behavior and his size. He'd grown used to it. Put it down to ignorance, phobia or just plain scared. But after sheltering Vivian and helping with little Joshua here, he figured it was about time she realized both he and Ma were harmless.

Of course, Ma had to pick that moment to scurry into the room, her hair as tangled as a crow's nest, her eyes wide. She paused to wave frantically at Vivian as if hoping her actions could chase her away. She mumbled something totally unintelligible before she darted past them and out to the lean-to to relieve herself.

He waited for her to return. He gave her a few minutes before he called, "Ma, get back in here."

Joshua, startled at Billy's loud voice, screamed as if he'd been stabbed. "Sorry, little fellow. Didn't mean to scare you." He rocked the baby.

Joshua stopped crying but his bottom lip stuck out, trembling, and his eyes remained wide.

Vivian jumped up. "I'll get a bottle ready."

Billy followed her to the table and waited while she

prepared breakfast for the baby. As soon as Vivian took Joshua, Billy headed for the cold woodshed attached to the house. He yanked open the door and caught Ma's hands, pulling her gently inside. "You'll freeze out there."

Ma whimpered and clung to his grasp. "I don't like this," she whispered. "It scares me."

"Ma, she's just a young woman with a little baby."

Ma shuddered and pressed one hand to her chest.

"Look, the storm has ended." He should be glad but it was not relief he felt. It was regret, which he expertly ignored as he led Ma to a kitchen chair. "You sit here while I get the fire going and make breakfast."

Only by talking softly of the animals and the weather did Billy manage to get Ma to sit long enough to eat. He took a bowl of hot mush to Vivian in front of the fireplace without suggesting she move to the table. He didn't want to risk sending Ma running from the room.

As soon as Ma finished, she started to pull on heavy outerwear. "I have to milk Betsy."

Billy pulled on his winter coat, too. "I'll look after the other animals." He lifted the bar off the door.

"Leave the dishes. I'll do them." Vivian spoke quietly.

Billy gladly did so and followed Ma to the barn where he hurried through his chores. He would normally take time to brush the colt, stroke all the cats and play with Limpy, his three-legged dog. Billy had nursed the pup from birth. He was the only dog left from many batches. Limpy was getting old. Billy would soon enough have to find a new dog, though the idea branded a protest on the inside of his heart.

Poor Limpy used to love this weather but he was getting old and refused to leave the barn unless it was warm out. Today, the cold had a nasty bite.

Ma milked Betsy. "You'll get rid of her today?"

"As soon as I've done the chores." The sooner the better for all of them. He'd struggle for weeks after she left to control the longings buried beneath the rubble in his heart, longings that had wormed their way to the surface during Vivian's visit.

"Good."

Ma finished milking and handed him the bucket. "I'll stay here until you leave."

"Ma, it's cold."

"I'll sit beside Betsy."

He hitched up Blaze. "I'll be back in a few minutes for the wagon. Will you go inside then?"

"Maybe." She gave him a look full of regret. "I'm sorry. I wish I didn't act so crazy when—"

"Never mind. We both know you aren't crazy."

She snorted. "How can you be so sure?"

"'Cause I know. Though you put up with me. Many would think that makes you crazy."

She smiled and brushed her mittens over his chin, the wool rough and damp smelling. "If they knew the truth, they would know I am blessed to have a son like you."

"Ma, I love you."

"And I you." She patted his cheek. "Look after the milk."

Billy laughed because the look she sent the direction of the house had nothing to do with milk, and everything to do with getting Vivian out of her house.

The cold made his cheeks tingle as he crossed the yard. He wondered about Vivian and Joshua. Bitter weather for them to be outdoors. He'd keep them another day if not for Ma.

As he strained the milk and fed the cats, he told Vivian they would leave in a few minutes. She had already packed everything into the basket and wrapped the baby. Obviously, she couldn't wait to get to town. It would never enter her mind to ask Billy to let her stay. A long-denied ache pooled low in his belly. No one would want to stay here with the crazy Blacks. He sucked in air until the ache disappeared. He didn't need or want anything more than what he had grown used to. His heart set on accepting the facts of his life, he returned to the barn.

"Ma, I want to see you back in the house before I leave. I don't want to have to worry you might freeze to death."

"As soon as she's gone."

"I'll wait at the bottom of the lane to see."

He drove the wagon to the door, grabbed a heavy

woolen blanket from the box and shook off cat hair. Vivian rushed out to meet him. She shivered in the penetrating cold and held the baby close to her chest under protection of the cape.

He grabbed the basket that held Joshua just yesterday. Still seemed impossible the soft-sided container kept the baby safe. He helped Vivian to the seat, and tucked the blanket tightly around her and the baby.

They started out. The drifts were hard but not impassable. They should make good time. He stopped at the bottom of the lane as he'd promised and turned back to the house, chuckling as Ma swept the step as if to remove all traces of this intrusion.

He kept his thoughts on the trail ahead as they turned onto the road. Within a few yards, they encountered a hard drift. Billy jumped down to stomp through it so Blaze could manage the wagon. The snow was deeper than he thought. He huffed from the effort. Should have a sleigh for this kind of journey. Would make more sense but he never had a need to go to town much in the winter and if he did, he rode Blaze.

He stopped twice more. The cold bit at his cheeks, nipped his fingertips. And he was working. Not sitting still like Vivian. She must be frozen clean through. And what about that little guy? He should never have brought them out. They could have stayed with the crazy Blacks until it warmed. He should have ignored her anxiousness to leave, he should have told Ma to settle down and wait for the cold to moderate. His thoughts twisted round and round each other like a tangle of ropes in a Dakota wind. If harm came to them… He couldn't think of it. Instead, he hurriedly broke the crust and led Blaze through the drift, lending his weight to the horse's efforts then climbed back to the seat. "How you doing?"

"Fine." The blanket she'd pulled over her head and across her face muffled her voice. Only her eyes peeked out and ice frosted her dark lashes.

"I ain't never took anyone out in this kind of cold." 'Course, he never took anyone anywhere. Not since the last time he took Ma to town and that was late fall with a warm sun, and…

He'd lost track of when it was, marking the seasons by the trees and the birth of foals and calves.

"The little one?"

"He's not moving much."

"He ain't?" He wanted to stop and fold back the covers, assure himself the baby hadn't been harmed by the cold, but until they found someplace warm it wouldn't be a good idea.

"The only warm place left in my body is where he is so I expect he's safe enough."

A whoosh of air escaped his mouth and he sucked in a big breath that stung his throat and practically froze his lungs. "We'll soon be there." Quinten lay down the road—a huddle of buildings covered with snow. Coils of gray smoke rose upward then bent to the south. "Hope the wind don't shift 'fore we get there."

Vivian grunted agreement.

They were but a few yards from town. He clenched his teeth until his jaw protested. He didn't usually go to town in the middle of the day. He didn't much care for the way women grabbed their children and ducked into the nearest doorway. "Where you want to go?" He'd see her to her destination and get out of town as fast as he could.

"To the Mercantile Bank."

He glanced about the approaching streets. Did he go boldly down the main street or turn aside to the alleys he usually used? Though he didn't have any call to visit the bank, it was close to Lucas's store. He made up his mind. "Don't mind if I don't go there directly?"

"Not at all." She lowered the blanket and looked about as eager as could be. "It's much the same as I remember." She craned to see down a street. "I lived down there," she whispered and shivered.

"Best wrap up. It's mighty cold." He had stopped feeling his feet several minutes ago. 'Course, he wasn't sure it was from cold or from the tension of this open visit to town.

But instead of pulling the blanket closer, she edged one arm out and touched her hair. "I must look a sight. I wish I had some place to clean up."

"'Spect the banker sees people come in looking

half-froze all the time." He'd meant to be amusing. But she didn't laugh. She looked at him with big appealing eyes.

"I'm not going to the bank to conduct ordinary business." Her teeth chattered. "Joshua's father works there. I am going to speak to him."

Billy took a moment to digest the information. He knew little about the bank except the news Lucas relayed, but he knew who owned it—the Styleses. Mr. Big Shot Daddy and his equally big shot son, Wayne—one of his tormentors in school and one of the most likely to cause Billy grief even now. Far as he knew, the only other person working in the bank was the elderly Mrs. Bamber. "You going to see one of the Styleses?"

She pulled the blanket around her head and mumbled, "Wayne."

The news hit him like a load of bricks dumped on his head, sending protests down his spine and tingling along his fingers. Wayne Styles was the father of that little baby?

"I know he wasn't fair to you in school. But he's changed. He was very nice to me when…"

When he got what he wanted and left you. But it wasn't his business.

They were almost at the bank. Vivian sat up straighter and stared at the imposing brick building. "I…" She turned to face him. "I don't want to say what I have to say in the bank. Can you keep the baby while I speak to him and arrange to meet someplace more private?"

He didn't want to do anything to help Wayne Styles but he couldn't resist the desperation in Vivian's gaze.

"Please. This is what's best for Joshua."

He made up his mind. "We need to get Joshua in out of the cold." There was one place he could go and he flicked the reins, passed the bank and drew up behind the store. Lucas would be some surprised to see him in broad daylight. He threw a blanket over Blaze and hurried around to assist Vivian to the ground. She stumbled as she tried to take her weight and he caught her.

"I'm okay," she mumbled, but she wasn't. Ignoring her protests, he scooped her up, pushed open the door and deposited her on a crate in the storeroom. He could hear Lucas talking to people in the front. The man would come to investigate the noise as soon as his customers left.

Billy fumbled at the blanket encasing Vivian, his fingers stiff with cold. Had to hurry. Had to make sure little Joshua... He folded back the blanket, parted the edges of the heavy woolen cape Vivian wore. More blankets covered the baby.

Shivering, her own movements clumsy with cold, Vivian lifted the covers to reveal the tiny face, eyes closed. He looked so peaceful. Too peaceful?

Vivian held her fingers a few inches from Joshua's

nostrils. "I can't tell if he's breathing." Her whispered words edged with fear.

Billy touched the baby's cheek. "He's warm." He planted his big hand on the tiny body and shook it. "Joshua. Wake up." Nothing. Not so much as a whimper. He shook again. "Joshua."

A pair of blue eyes flew open. And the baby smiled.

Billy grinned. "Hardy little critter."

Joshua nuzzled at Vivian's neck as she and Billy smiled at each other with their shared relief.

Her smile eased. Her gaze grew darker, more intense. She looked beyond his relief over the baby, past his enjoyment of that little smile, deep into the secrets of his heart, secrets he didn't admit even to himself and yet suddenly they lay bare and exposed, raw and unformed yet very real and alive. Like a newborn foal struggling to get to its feet. He tried to bar his thoughts but he couldn't. Instead, they poured forth, reaching for her with a force that both astounded and frightened him, one he was unable to restrain.

"Billy," she murmured.

He surged forward, ready to lift her in his arms and take her back to his home.

"Thank you for being such a help."

He sank back. "You're welcome." Big Billy Black with impossible dreams. What a laugh people would get if they could read his thoughts of a few seconds ago.

"What brings you out on a day so cold the air is

blue?" Lucas strode through the passageway and ground to a halt at the sight of a woman and child with Billy. He blinked as if hit by a blast of sunshine.

Billy grunted. He didn't have to act like the whole notion of Billy with a female friend was such a shock.

"Vivian, you remember Lucas Green?" Lucas was already working in the store when they were both in school. "Lucas, Vivian Halliday."

They exchanged greetings.

"How have you been, Miss Halliday?"

Vivian's smile was mocking. "Not bad, considering the circumstances."

Lucas fairly burst with curiosity, which neither Vivian nor Billy made any effort to satisfy.

"I have some business to conduct at the bank," Vivian said. She pulled a comb from the basket and looked around.

"Mirror over there." Lucas nodded toward the corner.

Vivian hesitated, her hands occupied with holding Joshua.

Billy reached for the baby who gave him a gummy smile. Realizing Lucas watched him openly, Billy settled the baby in the crook of his arm and pretended it was of no more importance than a bundle of papers. He got a perverse pleasure out of ignoring Lucas's questioning looks and furtive nods that invited information.

Vivian returned a few minutes later looking neat and tidy. "Do you mind watching him for a few minutes?"

"We'll be fine. You go about your business."

"He'll be wanting to eat soon, I expect. His bottle is in the bag."

"Fine."

She hesitated, her eyes filled with uncertainty.

He smiled, silently sending her encouragement. If this is what she wanted and what Joshua needed, he wished her all the best.

She patted Joshua's head and strode through the main part of the store.

Lucas barely waited for the door to close behind her. "So, what's going on?"

"I found them in the storm yesterday." Billy smiled, remembering his surprise, which had quickly shifted to pleasure. And now seemed to have turned into edginess at Lucas's curiosity and undisguised surprise. "She was returning to Quinten and got lost in the storm."

Lucas lapped up every word.

Billy let him drink eagerly and pant for more before he continued. "She's planning to start over here."

Lucas sat back. "She been with you overnight?"

Was that so hard to believe? "Yup."

"Your mother good with that?"

Billy chuckled. "Not quite."

Lucas shook his head. "Boy, you sure surprised me. Where's Vivian's husband?"

Billy didn't answer. It wasn't his place to spread tales about her. She'd face enough censure from the gossips without his help. But Lucas continued to stare, waiting for an answer.

"Can't say." It was the best he could do.

Joshua chose that moment to let them know he wanted to be fed. "Can I use your kettle?" Lucas kept a pot of water on the stove to add moisture to the air.

"Surely."

Billy set the bottle to warm. Ice crystals had formed along the edge so it took a few minutes.

Lucas joined him near the stove. "You and a baby. Never thought I'd see the day."

The man's amusement failed to annoy Billy. "I've looked after lots of animal babies. Human babies aren't a lot different." Except the animals didn't smile or curl their little hand around his smallest finger.

The entrance door to the store slapped open. A cold breeze skittered across the floor and Lucas reluctantly returned to his business.

The bottle ready, Billy sat back to feed Joshua, who sucked greedily. In a few minutes, Vivian would return to collect the baby. They would begin their new life. One in which Vivian would be respected as the wife of Wayne Styles.

The idea burned through his veins like his blood was on fire. He tried not to think of the two of them together—Vivian so sweet and gentle, and Wayne, a self-righteous bigot. Instead, he forced his thoughts to the family the three of them would become, the ideal family, welcomed, treated warmly, accepted.

Joshua smiled around the nipple, allowing milk to dribble down his cheek.

Billy chuckled as he wiped away the milk. Twenty-four hours since he'd met this young fella and yet there was a spot in a warm and sheltered part of his heart that now belonged to Joshua. A spot that would ache like Betsy had stomped on it with her sharp hooves when Vivian returned and took him away. "I'm going to miss you, little guy."

For just a moment, he wished his world could be different. Long ago, he'd accepted it couldn't be. But he'd do everything in his power to make sure Vivian and Joshua got the sort of life he wanted. Yet he found it hard to pray the words asking for Vivian's success in arranging a meeting with Wayne.

Chapter Five

Vivian's footsteps echoed on the wooden sidewalk. She wanted to walk to the bank with her head held high, revealing none of the nervousness tickling her ribs, but the wind caught at her and she ducked, shrugging deeper into the protection of her cape. Cold fingers caught at the edges of the garment and blasted it open. She tugged it closed and headed toward the bank.

Lord, God, please give me the confidence I need to face Wayne and make my request. Make him open to my need. Joshua's need.

Wayne had sugarcoated his words, tempting her, making their action seem so right. She knew better all the time. She had sinned, but she could not bear that Joshua would suffer rejection and indignities because of what she'd done. She counted on Wayne to make things right and had every assurance he would. He'd been such a gentleman when she saw him.

A horse plodded past, steam billowing from its nostrils, the rider bundled up in heavy clothing, a woolen cap beneath his cowboy hat.

Reassured by the commonplace event, she glanced about. But the drifting snow reduced visibility to half a block of businesses—several frame, false-fronted buildings and more brick and stone structures than she recalled. The town had changed and flourished since she last saw it. She played a mental game with herself as she scurried toward the bank, trying to recall what businesses she remembered—Mr. Legal's Law Office. She smiled. Never before thought of the irony of his name in conjunction with his occupation. The hotel farther down the street. The—

She reached the stone steps of the bank and ground to a halt. *Lord, God, help me.* Knowing God's way was the right way had started her on this journey. She strengthened herself with the thought as she climbed the steps and paused in front of the thick, leaded-glass doors to glance back toward the general store where her son waited, safe with Billy.

Billy was a good man. Kind enough to take her out in this treacherous weather. A smile curved her lips. Someday, perhaps she could repay his kindness.

Now to face her reason for returning to Quinten. She pushed the door open and stepped into the hushed, warm interior. She'd been in this building as a child and the same awe she'd felt then sucked at her courage.

The oiled-wood floors gave off a unique lemon

scent. The weary light shed soft muted tones to every-thing. Or perhaps the dark wood and yellow walls always made the interior feel that way.

An older woman with a coiled braid of white hair looked through the grate of the bank teller's cage and over the top of a pair of wire-rimmed glasses. She cleared her throat softly as if to suggest to Vivian that the woman awaited her business.

Vivian glanced about. In a side office, she saw an older man, a monk's bald spot the only part of his head visible. She wondered if it was Wayne's father. In a smaller office, another man, his suit jacket removed, fiddled with papers. She could not see Wayne. Perhaps he was in a back office.

After the woman behind the counter cleared her throat again, Vivian crossed toward her, resisting the urge to tiptoe.

"Can I help you, miss?"

Vivian refused to let the imperious tone of the woman's voice deter her. "I'd like to speak to Wayne Styles, please."

"And what is your business with him?"

"Would you please tell him Miss Halliday wishes to speak to him?"

The woman cleared her throat again. A most annoy-ing habit that grated across Vivian's tense nerves.

"I'm afraid I cannot do that." Another clearing of her throat. An upward tip of her chin as the woman studied Vivian through her reading glasses.

Although every nerve quivered with fear, Vivian would not give up. "Then I'd like to leave a message for him. Could I beg a piece of paper?"

The woman's gaze slipped past Vivian. Her eyelashes beat at a furious rate.

"Miss Halliday?" A male voice spoke behind her.

Vivian turned slowly, recognized the elder Mr. Styles with relief. "Thank goodness. Can you tell me how to contact Wayne? I need to speak to him."

"What is the nature of your concern? Perhaps I can help you?"

Vivian shook her head. "It's personal. I need to talk to Wayne myself."

The man looked as if the idea threatened all the money in his vault. "I'm afraid it isn't possible. Wayne is away."

"Away?" She'd never conceived of such a possibility. "Where? How long?"

"I don't see it's any of your concern but it's common knowledge he's gone east to visit relatives and friends."

"When is he due back?"

Mr. Styles sniffed. "I'm afraid I'm not at liberty to say. Now I believe any business we have with you has been concluded some time ago."

Vivian didn't realize he'd been shepherding her toward the exit until he reached it and waved her out. As the door closed behind her, she glanced back at the bank. Mr. Styles stood on the other side of the glass door, his expression far from friendly. She spun away, her heart frozen to the inside of her ribs.

Wayne was gone. What was she to do? She had no home. No family.

Ice edged her heart, immobilized her feet. She couldn't pull a single action from her scrambled brain.

"Vivian?"

She turned toward the sound. Billy? Her thoughts went no further.

"Come." He touched her elbow.

He wanted her to go with him. She understood that but her limbs didn't get the idea.

He caught her around the shoulders and steered her toward the store. And Joshua. Thinking of her son splintered her insides even more until she feared she'd disintegrate into a pile of kindling.

Billy pushed open the door, guided her through, past the shelves and counter and into the back room where Lucas sat holding her baby. He rose, and Billy steered her toward the vacant chair. Somehow she managed to fold her legs that felt like unwieldy stilts.

Billy took Joshua from Lucas and placed him in her arms.

She looked at the face of her son.

He smiled.

Her insides corrected themselves and with a strangled cry, she cradled Joshua to her chest.

"I'll leave you two alone." Lucas strode into the front of the store.

Billy squatted in front of her and with his thumbs swiped at her face, wiping away tears she wasn't even aware of shedding. "What happened?"

Vivian shook her head, unable to speak.

Billy nodded, seeming to understand. He stroked Joshua's head and patted Vivian's shoulder.

The tender gesture unlocked the tension inside her and she closed her eyes and sobbed silently.

Billy rubbed her shoulder, his silent acceptance of her tears releasing another rush of them. She cried until she was spent, her emotions drained. She found her hankie, dried her face and wiped her nose. A shudder shook her.

Billy squeezed her arm. "Better now?"

"Things couldn't be worse."

He held her gaze, his look soft and undemanding, silently offering nothing but kindness.

She searched his eyes, drawn by the intense blueness of them, drawn by something more, a deep understanding that likely stemmed from his own painful experiences. The realization that this man knew more about pain and disappointment than most released her fears. "Wayne isn't there. His father said he was away. Wouldn't tell me when he would be back." She cupped her hand to Joshua's head, pressing him to her chest. Her baby needed a father, a name, and acceptance.

Something Mr. Styles had said poked at the back of

her brain. She tried to recall his exact words. When she did, they made no sense.

"Mr. Styles said something odd. He said our business had been concluded some time ago. I don't know what he could mean."

Billy gave a one-sided grin. "He's a banker. All they think about is business."

"But I've had no business dealings with him. How could I? I was twelve when I went to the home."

"Perhaps he meant Joshua."

"I don't see how he'd know."

"Wayne doesn't know?" His voice seemed tight as if the man was some sort of scoundrel for not knowing.

"He returned home before I knew and I never informed him. Didn't seem the sort of thing to put in a letter." And then there were all those months of being the obedient Vivian Halliday who hid from the harsh realities of life by doing what she was told. She closed her eyes as pain and regret twisted through her. She had made a profound mess of her life. There was only one way to make it right. Tell Wayne. He would be expected to marry her since she had his son. That would make things right for Joshua, but Vivian would never forgive herself for her sinful behavior. Guilt grabbed every other emotion and squeezed it lifeless.

Except her love for Joshua. She would fight for his right to his father's name.

Lucas peeked into the room. "Everything all right?"

"Yes, thanks," Vivian said. Mr. Styles said something about everyone knowing Wayne was away. Maybe they also knew more about his plans than his father revealed. "Do you know when Wayne Styles will return?"

Lucas darted a look toward Joshua as if putting together her reason for wanting to know. "Nothing more than he's gone east to visit. Do you want me to let you know if I hear something?"

"I'd appreciate it." What was she to do in the meantime? She darted a look at Billy.

He considered her with a furrowed brow.

"There someplace I can take you?"

She thought of the people she remembered. Perhaps some of them would allow her to stay. But she didn't want anyone to know about Joshua until… Well, the more that knew the more censure there would be to overcome. Best if she could stay out of sight until Wayne returned and they could correct this shameful mistake in the only honorable way. Mrs. Weimer had a favorite saying. Stuck between the wagon and the mill wheel. Described Vivian's predicament perfectly. But she would do what she must. "Will you take me back with you and allow me to stay until he comes home?" He had every reason in the world to refuse. What would she do if he did?

Billy straightened. Backed away. Shifted his gaze to Joshua then he shook his head. Hard. "Can't do that. You know I can't."

"I have no place else."

Again he glanced at Joshua.

She wasn't above using his obvious affection for her son to persuade him, and turned Joshua around so Billy could see his face and silently thanked her little son that he picked that moment to smile and wobble a little fist. "I think it's the best thing for Joshua, don't you?"

Billy dragged his gaze back to Vivian's face. "You planning to hide forever?"

"Only 'til Wayne returns." She was grateful Lucas had returned to the main part of the store to wait on a customer. "Think about it. If everyone knows about Joshua before Wayne can do the right thing…well, you know how harmful gossip is and how difficult to live down." It was an unfair argument considering Billy's experience, but surely he would realize how important it was that she shield Joshua.

A muscle in Billy's jaw bunched. He curled his fists into knotted mounds of power, then he nodded briskly. "You and Ma will have to figure out how to get along. Now, let's get going."

He spoke a moment to Lucas. She overheard Billy ask him to keep Vivian's presence quiet for now.

She smiled. Billy understood. She could trust him to protect her secret. And protect her, as well, she realized with a start.

They left town in a swirl of snow.

Billy had said she would have to get along with his ma. She wondered how she was expected to do that.

She didn't know what she shouldn't do in order to prevent sending the mad Mrs. Black out of control. Nor could she guess what sort of action she'd precipitate by something even seemingly innocent.

She shuddered, and pulled the blanket tighter around her as if she could protect herself from more than the cold with the thick wool.

The temperature had dropped significantly since their earlier trip to town. She ducked her head. The cold sucking at her made everything else—including the specter of being stuck with the mad Blacks—fade into the distance.

It was, she admitted, only Mrs. Black that caused this itchy edginess to her insides. She didn't fear Billy. She recalled the strength of his arms holding her, giving her a sense of safety and protection. He was a man who would help her to his own cost. A man who would stroke a cat gently, rock a baby and sing to settle the fretful cries, a man who...

She closed her thoughts to visions of Billy's big hands comforting away her fears. She buried her nose in the blanket and breathed in the smell of horseflesh.

The cold bit at her through the heavy blanket and she hunkered lower to protect Joshua. Nothing mattered more than keeping this infant safe.

By the time they arrived back at the Black homestead, the only warm spot was in the middle of her chest where the baby lay. She literally fell into Billy's arms and he rushed inside.

His mother jerked to her feet. "You brought her back?"

"Had to."

"I don't want her here." She waved her arms like a scarecrow caught in a whirlwind.

A bolt of fear went halfway through Vivian's heart before the frozen crust around her emotions stalled it. Not even Mrs. Black's madness mattered at the moment. All she cared about was getting warm.

Billy gently lowered her to the chair, paused to throw more wood on the fire then slowly unwrapped her. He pried Joshua from her stiff arms. "Ma, see to the baby."

"No." She sucked back a cry. "I'll not be touching anyone's baby."

Billy straightened. "Then go take care of Blaze. Put the kettle to boil before you leave. Vivian needs warming."

The heat from the fire touched Vivian but her skin seemed impervious. She couldn't remember being so cold. Not even when she'd thought she was going to die in the storm. A good deal of the chill came from inside, near her heart, as if an iceberg had found its way into her thoughts and feelings. She had not expected this delay. She couldn't have imagined how it caused her to feel so helpless. Knowing she was unwelcome here only intensified her sense of loss and confusion until she welcomed the way her thoughts had grown immobile with the cold.

Billy opened the blankets covering Joshua. He shook the baby gently and smiled when Joshua squalled. "You're a tough little man." He glanced toward the ceiling. "Thank You, God."

Vivian made a noise—somewhere between a grateful grunt and a cry of pain. She echoed his prayer of gratitude adding, *Please keep us safe*.

Billy carefully pulled her boots off and squeezed her toes. "Do you feel this?"

Her toes hurt—a good sign. She managed to mumble something she hoped sounded like yes. He pulled off her mittens. Her fingers hurt, too.

Billy grabbed a blanket from a pair roasting near the fireplace. He pushed back the snow-dusted one she'd huddled in and covered her with the new one. "You'll be okay as soon as you get warm."

He went to make tea, then returned to sit at her knees and lifted a spoonful toward her. "It'll warm you up quick."

At his gentleness, tears built up behind her eyes and stalled there. Even her tear ducts were so cold they refused to work.

"Here." He pressed the spoon against her lips and she opened her mouth. The warm liquid slid down her throat but did little to relieve the frigid state of her insides. The cold winding around her heart had nothing to do with the temperature in her body, and everything to do with the aloneness she'd lived with since her parents died.

"More." He continued, spoonful after spoonful of warm, sweet tea until the cup was empty. Each time his big hand brushed her mouth, she reminded herself he was only treating her as he would any of his pets if they needed special attention.

Slowly, in painful increments, feeling returned to her limbs. She wished the numbness could remain in her heart but feeling seeped back there, as well, making her keenly aware of her state. She tried not to think about the facts of her life, stuck where she wasn't welcome, with a baby out of wedlock and Wayne away.

Mrs. Black stomped back into the house. "I took care of your horse."

Billy put aside the cup. "Did you make dinner? I'm starved."

"I won't be cooking for strangers."

He snorted. "I'm not hardly one."

She glowered. "You'll find your food in the oven."

"Thanks, Ma."

Vivian closed her eyes. She didn't want to be here any more than Mrs. Black wanted her. But what choice did she have? "I'm sorry, Mrs. Black. I desperately need shelter." It wasn't even for herself she sought it but for tiny, defenseless Joshua.

The woman turned her back and spoke to Billy. "Ain't she got kin?"

"She's an orphan."

"Huh. Ain't she got friends?"

"She needs a place to stay."

"Not here."

"Yes, Ma. Here. Just for a time."

Vivian hoped and prayed it would be a very short time. She pushed to her feet, grimacing as pins and needles jabbed up her legs. "I won't bother you."

"Ain't cooking for uninvited guests," Mrs. Black informed Billy as she poured a cup of tea and sat at the table, keeping her back to Vivian.

When Joshua loudly announced he needed to be fed, Vivian dug the bottle out of the basket, her fingers clumsy with cold.

Seeing her predicament, Billy took over.

She gratefully sank back to the rocker. It would be some time for proper feeling to return to her limbs.

A few minutes later, Billy lifted Joshua into her arms and handed her the bottle. She turned to thank him and realized he still bent over admiring Joshua, their faces almost touching. For the first time, she noticed the way his cheeks creased as if his mouth curved in permanent amusement. He was so close she could smell the metallic scent of cold from his skin. And ache for the comfort his arms offered.

She mentally scolded herself. Hadn't she learned her lesson about looking to a man for comfort? She'd promised never again. *Lord, God, forgive me for being so needy. Give me strength.*

Billy ambled to the stove to pull out a fry pan heaped with food. He dug into it with gusto and devout concentration. Not until he'd cleaned the pan did he look up. "You must be hungry."

Before Vivian could answer, Mrs. Black skidded her chair back, the sharp noise jerking along Vivian's nerves.

Vivian shook her head. "I'm fine." Though the cold had burned off breakfast and probably a few meals prior.

Billy sawed off two thick pieces of bread, spread them with molasses, put them on a plate and took them to Vivian. "It might tide you 'til supper."

Mrs. Black bounced her chair back to the table. "Ain't cooking."

Billy shrugged. "Then you all will have to put up with my form of cooking."

Vivian smiled in spite of her nervousness. "Supper last night was more than adequate."

His face broke into a sunny expression, smile lines fanning out from his eyes and mouth. "That was the extent of my ability."

Vivian glanced at Mrs. Black and lowered her voice. "I could cook."

Billy's eyebrows pushed furrows up his forehead. "Good. But—" He paused and his eyes crinkled in what she took as embarrassment. "I ain't a dainty eater."

She chuckled, keeping her voice low. She'd already noticed the fact but didn't think it would be kind to say so. "You show me the food and I'll concoct something to satisfy."

"I'll do that as soon as the little feller is done with his dinner."

Joshua finished eating and Vivian settled him in the chair then followed Billy to the pantry. He opened bins and showed her where things were, then led her to the cold woodshed attached to the house. A slab of some animal hung under a gunnysack shroud.

"I'll cut off a hunk of meat. What would you like?"

Vivian did some figuring. It was early afternoon yet. "A nice big roast."

She waited for him to saw it off and followed him back to the kitchen. When Mrs. Black saw she intended to work at the stove, she made a sharp sound of protest and jerked to her feet, crossing the room to settle in the rocker, favoring Vivian with dark glances.

Vivian's instinct was to keep her back to the woman and ignore her but when she did, her skin tightened. Better the enemy you could see than one you couldn't, so she turned. As she put the roast in the oven then prepared potatoes and turnips, Mrs. Black glowered relentlessly at her. Having no desire to sit in front of the fire and move the staring match into close quarters, Vivian went to the pantry and found dried apples and enough ingredients for a German apple pudding cake— something she'd learned to make at the Weimers'.

Billy had gone back to the woodshed and now returned with a crate lined with fur. "I made Joshua a little bed."

His mother whimpered.

Billy ignored her, and Vivian tried her best to do likewise as she went to examine the little nest he'd made.

"It's very nice. The baby will be warm and safe here." She thought of picking up Joshua and seeing how he fit, but Mrs. Black's dark look halted her at first thought.

Seeing her hesitation, Billy murmured, "She ain't gonna hurt you."

How could he be so certain? Vivian kept her face expressionless. Just because the woman had never hurt him didn't guarantee she would not hurt someone who seemed to step on her toes simply by being in the room.

Billy put Joshua in the box. The baby snuffled a bit and returned to sleeping.

Vivian smiled. "Thank goodness he isn't screaming like he did last night."

The pair of them hung over the box for a moment, watching Joshua sleep, but one could stare at a sleeping baby only so long. Vivian returned to the kitchen. Billy settled in the stuffed chair and opened the newspapers he'd brought from town. Mrs. Black glowered at the paper hiding her son's face then stomped to the quilt frame. She perched on a stool and bent over the quilt, studiously stitching the layers together.

"You want to read the news?" Billy offered Vivian a paper.

Grateful for the diversion, she glanced at the headlines, which held no interest for her. Her own problems were enough to contemplate without examining the troubles of others. She found the current serial and read the latest escapades of the pair in the story, chuckling aloud at the predicaments they got themselves into. When Mrs. Black made an angry sound, Vivian choked back her amusement.

As the light began to fade, Vivian put the vegetables to cook. A little later she announced, "Supper's ready."

Billy hurried to the table but Mrs. Black acted as if she hadn't heard.

"Ma, suppertime."

The woman shook her head and made a high-pitched sound of refusal or anger. Vivian had no way of knowing which.

Billy hesitated, his gaze devouring the food. "You got to eat. And it looks mighty good."

Still, Mrs. Black did not move.

Billy grabbed a chair and pulled it out. He hesitated again, seemed puzzled about what to do with his mother. Then he sat. "I guess it's up to you whether or not you eat but I intend to enjoy this." He tipped his head toward another chair, indicating Vivian should sit.

She didn't move. "I can wait. Let your mother eat."

The woman jumped to her feet. A pair of scissors

clattered to the floor as she dashed to the pantry and again disappeared into the far corner.

Billy sighed. "Let's give thanks. Good Lord, bless these sinners as they eat their dinners. Amen."

A bubble of amusement tickled Vivian's throat. She tried to choke it back. After all, one didn't laugh about a prayer. But had he meant to be poking fun at the situation or was he being naively sincere? She stole a look from under her eyelashes, saw a twinkle in his eyes informing her he did it on purpose. She could no longer contain it and sputtered with laughter.

He grinned as he filled a plate and took it to his ma, then piled another almost as high as his chin. He ate several mouthfuls, came up for air long enough to say, "Good supper," then cleaned his plate. His eyes rounded with appreciation when she served a generous portion of the dessert topped with cream so thick she'd piled it on with a spoon. "Ma is gonna really like this." He took her a dishful. "Look, Vivian made dessert."

The woman mumbled something in an angry tone but Vivian noticed Billy did not bring the food back.

They did the dishes together then, as he'd done the night before, Billy drew his mother from the pantry to the fireplace. Joshua wakened and Vivian sat on a kitchen chair to feed him, listening as Billy read again from the Bible.

He read for some time, his voice calming his mother.

A little later, Mrs. Black rose and went to her room,

not saying a word or making any unearthly noises, but closing the door firmly behind her.

"I have to tend to something." Billy went in and out of the woodshed and back and forth to the doorway next to his mother's room.

Vivian paid him little mind. After all, the man no doubt had things that needed doing.

"I've fixed my room for you."

"I couldn't. Where will you sleep? Besides, I'm fine here." But every bone in her body ached to stretch out and relax.

"I put up a cot in the other room for me. It's supposed to be a bedroom but we haven't needed it so it's gotten used for storage." He snorted. "A junk collection, really."

She wanted to refuse but truthfully she ached for a proper sleep. The baby woke, boisterously demanding to be fed, and she was saved from trying to find a way to refuse his offer.

He prepared the bottle and handed it to her. As Joshua settled down to sucking greedily, Billy sank into the other chair. "How did you get messed up with Wayne?"

His question hammered through her thoughts, drove spikes into her heart. How, indeed?

Chapter Six

She would have avoided the question but Billy's patient expression suddenly made her want to explain. "I don't know where to start."

He shrugged. "Does it matter where you start? Sooner or later you'll end up at the same place."

His attitude made her relax. "When I was fifteen, I was sent to work at the Weimers'. They owned a feed store, ran a gristmill and grain farm. There were always men to feed, customers to serve and the house and buildings to keep clean."

"Did you like it?"

"What? Working at the Weimers'?" His question startled her. "It didn't matter what I liked. I had no choice about where I went or what I did. An orphan has no say." How well she'd learned to live by that truth.

"Did they treat you right?"

His words slammed straight through the complacent attitude she had adopted after her few unsuccessful rebellions at the home. She'd quickly learned life was much easier if she asked no questions, made no demands. But behind her acceptance lay a sea of hurt. She had no choice about where she went and no one to care if she was treated kindly or otherwise. Thankfully, his words only skimmed the surface of that vast expanse.

"They were fair enough. If I did my work they didn't bother me much."

"Much? What does that mean?"

"They expected obedience, and quickly. A person learned not to dilly-dally around. They would tolerate no rudeness to them or the customers. But they didn't use the strap for no reason. Nor did they let the customers take advantage of me. They were decent people." Her obedient attitude had served her well. Yet all the time, the hunger for more—more being seen, being valued, being somebody—grew until her hunger for approval made her easy prey to her feelings when Wayne appeared on the scene.

"Wayne had business in the area. We recognized each other immediately. He spent several weeks conducting his business. I saw him every day. And soon—"

"What was his business?"

Her thoughts stalled. Somehow, his reason for being there had never come up. "I don't know. He never

exactly said." They'd discussed other things. Done
other things. Her cheeks grew hot with shame. Certain
Billy could see the brilliant red of her thoughts, her
regrets, she lowered her gaze. In her arms lay the
evidence of her sin—Joshua. But for nine months—
more if she considered the two he'd been in the foundling home—her love for him had grown until it
almost swallowed up the shame of her sin. Almost.

She wanted to explain although she knew she was
without excuse. "When Wayne showed up it was like
a bit of home had been given back to me. I remember
Wayne at school." She lifted her gaze to Billy. "I know
he was unkind. Not only to you. But he grew up.
Changed."

His eyes remained hard and unyielding as if he
didn't believe her.

"He brought me little gifts—some candy, a new
hankie with lace and—" Of course Billy didn't care
about the fine hankie. Nor would he understand how
important Wayne's gifts had seemed. "He took me to
church. To a literary evening." How wonderful it had
been to have an escort, to feel like someone cared that
she'd fixed her hair special. No matter that she had
only the plain gray dress the Weimers provided. She
tried her best to fancy it up by folding the hanky into
a fan and pinning it to her bodice. Wayne had noticed
and said how nice it looked.

"We went for long walks. He told me how Quinten
had changed, reminded me of the people I'd known. I

thought…" She'd been so foolish to build dreams and plans on his words. "I thought he meant…" she swallowed hard "…to take me with him."

She pushed aside her shame, her regrets, her sense of having been a fool. "Otherwise…" She couldn't bring herself to give her awful sin a name. "I wouldn't have done it."

"But he never knew. When he sees Joshua he will do what any honorable man would do. He'll marry you."

She nodded. "And give Joshua a home and a name."

"Lucas will get a message to us when Wayne returns." His blue eyes revealed his weariness with the subject and lots more besides.

She thought she detected sadness, and likely an echo of the same shame creasing permanent pinpoints of pain into her brain.

He shifted to stare at the flames. As if he couldn't bear to look at her anymore.

She didn't blame him. Her own mirror threw back an unforgiving, condemning glance. Only one thing enabled her to face the present and contemplate the future—Joshua. Besides the baby, one other good thing had come of the situation. She'd learned to pray—urgent, soul-filled prayers—and her faith had grown strong. She could trust God to see her through this complication.

"He ever do any business that you know of?"

The sudden shift of focus stalled every thought. "I

don't recall." Suddenly, she remembered the paper she'd signed. "I did give my signature to a form. He said it was a formality to close the debt my parents owed."

Billy's head cranked around. "Did the bank sell the house?"

"Yes, of course, but they didn't get enough from the sale. I think Wayne wanted to do me a favor and cancel the debt. He said there was no need for me to worry about clearing my parents' name."

"Huh. First time I heard of the Styleses forgiving a debt."

She gave a smile that felt like it struggled with the corners of her mouth. "Perhaps because he had some fondness for me."

"Could be." But his expression tightened even more.

She understood he and Wayne might have ongoing problems.

"What happened when you realized…?" He didn't need to finish his question for her to know what he meant.

Shame. Condemnation. "The Weimers allowed me to stay. Once I couldn't hide my condition, I had to stay out of sight of their customers." Not a day passed when the Weimers didn't remind her of her disgrace. Not that she needed it. Her own heart condemned her. Though after the first fluttering kicks of her baby, a love so profound she couldn't comprehend it had competed with the voice of shame.

"They let you stay after the baby was born?" He had reason to sound surprised.

Her insides wrenched as shame, regret, pain all twisted inside her until she wondered if her heart would burst. "You have to understand something about me. I was weak. I let people tell me what to do. I didn't think I had any choice."

He looked at her full on, quietly waiting for her to continue.

She couldn't break from his gaze even as self-condemnation made the skin around her eyes feel brittle. Something about the way his look seemed full of kindness such as she hadn't seen in a long time made her want to tell him everything, as if by speaking the truth she could rid herself of the guilt. She knew it wouldn't happen but yet a little bit of her hoped.

"I learned early to do what I was told in order to avoid punishment or a reminder of my precarious state as an orphan. When it was time for me to have Joshua, the Weimers sent me back to the home. As soon as the baby was born, they took him away. You see, unmarried orphan girls can't keep their babies and everyone says it's best if they don't see them. They wouldn't even tell me if it was a boy or a girl." She could barely squeeze the whispered words past the spasm in her throat. "I was allowed to rest for a week and then sent back to work." The first few days were a blur of physical and mental pain, of a sense of loss and failure like nothing she could imagine. Her body reminded her daily of the birth and the fact she had nothing to show for it but the cramps in her belly.

It was weeks before she could think at all without crying, though she learned quickly not to cry when anyone could see her.

She was totally unaware she cried now until a tear dripped from her chin. She swabbed at her cheeks with a corner of Joshua's blanket.

"I only knew I had a son because my friend Marie cared for the babies in the home." She paused as another wave of pain engulfed her. "He was supposed to be adopted."

He nodded, his look so intent she felt as if she were wrapped in his thoughts. Kind thoughts. It was a surprising idea and one that eased some of the tension mounting as she told her story.

"I thought of Joshua every day. I prayed for him. And slowly, I grew strong enough to start thinking."

A slow smile filled his eyes. "And you ain't stopped since."

She chuckled. "I started to think how I could provide a home for Joshua myself. All it would take was finding Wayne. So I... You might not want to hear this part."

He chuckled. "You stole the baby from his new parents? I can see you doing it."

"No one had adopted him. Can you imagine?"

They both studied Joshua who sucked one fist and kicked his legs.

"Can't. No."

"Thank you." They exchanged a smile full of sweet-ness. It was good to share her love for Joshua with someone even if only temporarily. "I told the Weimers I was leaving. They weren't too pleased. I guess they appreciated my work though not once did they say so. I told a little lie. I said Wayne had sent for me. It was the only way I figured they'd let me go."

"Guess it ain't the worst thing a person could do."

"No. I'd already done worse." She held his gaze, wondering if he would reveal disgust.

Instead, he grinned. "I'm having a hard time think-ing Joshua is wrong."

It was the kindest thing anyone could say and she hugged her son, though what she wanted to do was hug Billy.

She returned to her story. "I made my way back to the home. Marie helped me even though she was prob-ably whipped for it. She let me know when Matron— that's what we called the head of the home—and her assistants were busy elsewhere and then she let me in to get Joshua. It was the first time I'd ever held him." She couldn't go on.

Billy leaned forward and squeezed her fingers. She turned her palm into his, let his big fist swallow her hand. His strength filled her.

She smiled. "Remember you asked if a lawman would be after you?"

"Wondering even more now."

"I have his birth certificate saying I'm his mother. Marie said that would be proof enough if Matron happened to send the law after me."

"Good to know." He squeezed her hand again and withdrew, leaving her feeling alone.

"So, here I am."

"Yes, here you are. Until Wayne returns."

She blinked. For a moment, she'd forgotten Wayne. She felt safe here. Except when Mrs. Black was up. "I hope it won't be long."

Billy's expression grew tight, his eyes guarded. "You and Ma both. Is the little guy ready for bed?"

Joshua chewed on his fist and showed no sign of being sleepy.

"I'll give him another bottle in a little while then put him down. Don't let us keep you up."

He lumbered to his feet. "I'll say good-night, then." He ducked into the narrow doorway and closed the door quietly.

Vivian let out a long, shaky sigh. For a few minutes, she'd thought Billy might care about how she fared and then suddenly he'd withdrawn. She couldn't blame him. She was a woman with a sinful past—a past that couldn't be hidden.

A little later, Joshua cried and she prepared his bottle, relaxing as he sucked back his milk. She burped him, changed him and tucked him into the fur-lined bed. He stiffened and screamed.

She picked him up again and tried to burp him. But Joshua arched his back and wailed. She wrapped him tighter and walked back and forth, jostling the baby. But he wouldn't settle. Was this his normal nighttime behavior? His crying seemed full of distress. Had he gotten too cold on the trip to town and back? Maybe he was sick or hurting. How did one know with such a little baby?

Billy strode into the room, his curls more unruly than usual. He wore hastily donned trousers with suspenders over his woolens. "Fussy again?"

"I don't know. Maybe he's sick or hurt."

"Is he hot?"

She pressed her cheek to the baby. "He's warm and damp."

"Probably from too much crying. Here, let me take him."

She gladly gave him the squalling bundle and returned to the rocker.

Billy cradled the baby on his barrel-sized chest and walked the floor.

He hummed as he walked and slowly the baby stopped fussing. He continued to walk for fifteen minutes then eased down into the stuffed chair.

"How do you do that?" she asked.

"I don't know. But be happy it works."

"I am. I'm also annoyed he won't settle in my arms. What am I doing wrong?"

"He's just a baby. He doesn't make judgments.

Probably has a tummy ache. Maybe my voice calms him."

"Then you better keep talking."

She invited him to talk? To sit and talk to her? Him. Big Billy Black. The monster of the county.

Warmth flared through him.

He looked at the fire to see if a log had burst open releasing an explosion of heat, but the flames simmered gently. The heat came from inside his own chest, bursting forth from a long-forgotten, always-denied spot, a spot he purposely neglected, where companionship and acceptance were normal.

Not that he needed anyone to talk to. He said plenty—to his pets, to the patient, good Lord up above and to the air. But within the space of a day, he'd discovered it wasn't the same as having someone with flashing brown eyes to acknowledge his words or challenge him with questions.

She'd be gone quick enough, though. He'd be back to having the cats, the good Lord and the clouds up above to talk to. Best not get used to eyes and mouth in a lively face. He would return to being alone, Big Billy Black.

But he'd had none of these rational arguments when Lucas called to say she stood in the middle of the sidewalk. Hadn't moved in several minutes. He hadn't even considered someone might see him as he rushed to her side.

When she'd told about becoming Joshua's mother, how the baby had been sent to a foundling home, his insides had practically caved in. He sensed her pain and helplessness. He didn't know what it was like to be an orphan but he knew too much what it felt like to be treated like he had no feelings. His insides curled with anger that she should have endured such unkindness. Nor was it over. The future would carry its share of whisperings even after she married Wayne, though being a Styles would protect her as much as anything. He tried not to let it bother him to think of her marrying that man.

The baby snuffled. He patted the wee mite and made a low sound. The baby squirmed. "Guess he needs to hear my voice." He hankered to know more about Vivian and saw no need to waste a perfectly good opportunity. "What was it like when your ma and pa were alive?"

Her face softened in remembrance.

"We lived a simple life. Father was a carpenter. He made nice things for the house. He made me a beautiful dollhouse for my eighth birthday. I wonder what happened to it?" She stared into the distance. "Over the sofa were pictures in matching frames of Blue Boy and Pinkie. I liked to sit on a footstool looking at them as my mother read to me."

"You felt special as a child."

"I did. Didn't you?"

He closed his mind. "I prefer not to look back."

"Surely there must be good things to remember? I'm not meaning to pry but I'm… I guess I'd like to understand what happened to you."

How could she possibly begin to understand? His thoughts slid back to before—before everything turned upside down. Yet amid the bad things, he found surprising flashes of things special and comforting. He plucked the most vivid. "We lived in a tiny house, a settler's shack, on the edge of Indian territory. I remember picking berries with Ma. I 'spect I was eating more than went in my bucket. I recall how they were both sweet and tart. Ma said she'd make me a pie and maybe jam. She hugged me and laughed. Said she wouldn't kiss me 'cause I was sticky with berry juice. The sun was warm. I felt special that day.

"I'd plumb forgot about it. It was before—" He broke off. He didn't talk about before. Didn't think on it more'n he was forced to.

"Before? Do you mean before—"

"Ma's capture?"

"I'm sorry. It's none of my business."

"Hmm. Seems like everybody's made it their business."

"I'm sorry," she said again. "I don't mean to be curious, but how old were you when…?" She tipped her head toward Ma's door.

Billy shifted the baby a little, righted the tiny head, all the time holding Vivian's warm brown gaze. Something about the way she studied him, waiting, a little fearful perhaps, a little curious but maybe, just maybe, feeling a need to explore something they'd shared— the loss of a mother. Fear of what people would say. So many painful things came from the lips of people who seemed to have no compassion. She'd lost her father, too. For her, they would never return. Suddenly, he wanted to tell her how it was. How things could change. How life didn't stay the same. Though he guessed she knew that and expected to find a different future when Wayne returned.

"I was six years old when Ma was captured. She saw the Indians coming and hid me behind the wood in a cupboard much like that." He pointed to the cavity filled with firewood. "I was already a big boy. I don't know how she managed to put the wood back in good enough to hide me. She made me promise not to make a sound no matter what happened. I heard her scream and then it grew quiet. I didn't move until I heard Pa calling us." He stopped and took a deep breath. "She saved my life."

"How awful for you."

He shut away the pain—that was then—and focused on the contentment of now. "Not knowing if she was dead or alive was the worst. Pa said he thought she was dead. I heard him tell someone he prayed she was. When I heard that, I ran into our little root cellar and cried. I didn't want my ma to be dead. Then I got used to her being gone. She was gone six whole years."

Vivian's eyes glistened. "I can't imagine what she went through. It's no wonder—"

"She's crazy? Only she isn't. Just scared." He shifted the baby and when the little one didn't waken, put him into the bed he'd made. "He's settled, and I think we both need to get some sleep." As he headed for the door, Vivian touched his arm.

"Your mother is fortunate to have you."

Startled, he stopped and looked down at her. Remembering the berry-picking time before his mother's capture had enlivened a yearning long buried, long denied. Vivian's touch gave it power to burn upward to his heart where it gave a solid, insistent beat, then it headed straight to his eyes, making them sting with embarrassed heat. He blinked twice, grateful she hadn't noticed the awkward pause. "I'm fortunate to have her."

Chapter Seven

Billy pulled the covers to his chin. His suddenly exposed feet protested the cold. He shifted, adjusted his bulk, trying to find the usual comfortable spots in his mattress. But he'd given his bed to Vivian and this one wasn't big enough to accommodate his size. He groaned as he remembered the night before, how he'd let down a barrier in his mind and told Vivian about Ma. Something he'd kept to himself all these years.

He snorted in derision. Not that everyone didn't know, or fill in the details as they wished.

But only Pa knew he'd hidden while his ma was captured. He was only a boy and couldn't have stopped the Indians. He understood Ma would have suffered more if her son had been captured, too. Nevertheless, knowing didn't change the feeling he'd let her down.

No matter what was done or what people said, it wouldn't happen again. He would take care of Ma.

He'd protect her from every kind of danger—physical or otherwise.

It was time to get up and he tossed aside the inadequate covers, yanked on his clothes and hurried from the icy room.

Vivian, dark shadows under her eyes, sat in front of the fire, rocking Joshua.

He hadn't heard the baby but she looked as if she hadn't slept. "He didn't fuss all night, did he?" He should have stayed up longer. Seems little Joshua would only settle for him. His chest expanded. He kind of liked knowing that.

"He slept some. He's just had another bottle and he's gone back to sleep." She put the baby in his little bed. "I'll get breakfast started."

Ma scurried from her room, jerked on her coat and boots, grabbed the milk pail and headed outside.

Vivian hung back until Ma left. "I don't mean to frighten her."

"It's not your fault. She doesn't like strangers." He pulled on his heavy coat and fur hat. "I'll feed the critters. Give you time to cook up a feed." He put a slight emphasis on the last word hoping she would make enough to fuel him for a few hours.

She laughed. "I've cooked for large crews. I think I can manage to make enough food to satisfy your appetite."

He grinned widely. "I don't eat quite as much as a threshing crew."

She lifted her eyebrows in a flash of disbelief. "Guess it depends on the size of the crew."

She was teasing. He could tell by the way her eyes seemed to capture the light seeping through the window and hoard it. He knew by the way the corners of her mouth tilted upward just enough to round her cheeks. And knowing it felt as if the spring butterflies had returned but instead of fluttering at the trees, they danced in his heart. A chuckle started slow and cautious in the pit of his stomach. It rolled, building up volume and speed until it burst from his throat, spilling out in deep, satisfying explosions.

His pleasure deepened when she laughed softly then said, "I'll do my best."

He still chuckled as he entered the barn.

Ma looked up. "What's so funny?"

"Vivian. She said she could make enough food for me 'cause she's cooked for crews. She was teasing me about my big appetite."

"Huh. Don't you be getting fond of that woman. She won't stay. She'll go and maybe…"

The knowledge sobered Billy and stole the pleasure of his amusement. "Is that what you're afraid of? That some woman will come along and persuade me to leave?"

Ma turned away but not before he caught the dark fear in her eyes.

"That will never happen."

"You ain't going to be happy with me the rest of your life."

"I'd never leave you. You know that."

They fell silent, but her words edged into his thoughts and poked unwelcome fingers into secret places. It might be nice to have someone like Vivian to laugh with. But like Ma said, no one would live out here. No one would ever be comfortable around Ma. Or maybe it was she who would never be comfortable around someone else, and would do her best to drive them away. He sighed. What did it matter? He had all he wanted right here—the mother he'd been deprived of as a child, his animals and the great outdoors. God's gifts were sufficient. He would not acknowledge his loneliness that had a Vivian shape to it.

He fed the cats, played with Limpy who needed little else but a pat on the head, put out some oats for Betsy's latest calf, already half grown, and gave Blaze a good brushing. He wanted to spend some time alone talking to the animals and collecting his thoughts, but Ma finished and waited for him. He sighed. She wouldn't return to the house without him. Not with Vivian there.

He put away the currycomb and left the barn.

The cold had a snap to it. He didn't need a thermometer to know the temperature had dipped to a new low. Despite the cold, it was beautiful outdoors. Even though his nose stung by the time they crossed the yard, if he didn't have to hang around the house for

Ma's sake, he might have considered a walk to the creek just to see how it looked frozen over and snow dusted.

He stepped inside, and sucked in delicious smells of sausage, cinnamon, hot fat and coffee. Saliva flooded his mouth and a loud growl came from his stomach. It didn't take him a full minute to scramble from his outer clothes. He hurriedly washed his hands then sat at the table, greedily eyeing the stacks of food. A pile of griddle cakes, a bowl of hot applesauce, a heap of sausages, a steaming pot of thick porridge. "I see you found the rest of the supplies."

"You have enough to feed a small army."

He chuckled at the teasing in her voice. "Or one large man. Ma, you gonna sit down so we can eat?"

She shot him a look full of accusation and ducked into the pantry. Seems she'd decided to eat all her meals in solitude. "Suit yourself." He waggled a finger toward a chair, indicating Vivian should join him. His stomach growled demandingly.

She laughed. "We better hurry."

He bowed his head. "Lord, bless this food we are about to receive and bless the hands that prepared it." He grinned at Vivian when he raised his head, pleased at the gentle blush in her cheeks.

Ma made a sharp noise of protest and he rolled his eyes. Vivian giggled, increasing his pleasure. Billy needed no invitation to dig in. He filled his mouth before he took a plate to Ma. He didn't bother waiting for her to say anything before he hurried back to his food.

Several minutes later, he paused. "Good food."

"Thanks."

"Where'd you learn to cook?"

"From Mrs. Weimer. She insisted I learn many of her German dishes."

"Awfully glad she did."

"Good. If you're stuck with me, I can at least do something useful."

He chuckled. "You keep cooking like this and I might be tempted to keep you."

Ma muttered.

He raised his voice. "I'm joshing, Ma."

Unappeased, Ma stomped from the pantry. He'd never seen her quite so angry and determined. She deposited her used dishes, then hurried to the stool by the quilt and picked up her needle. The way she jabbed it into the material made Billy feel like laughing. Ma wanted him to understand she wouldn't let him keep Vivian.

As if she'd stay.

He couldn't successfully ignore the silent cry that wished she would. Somehow, he forced his face to be expressionless as he turned back to Vivian. "Thank you for breakfast."

"It's me who should be thanking you for allowing me to remain here."

Ma grunted.

Billy shook his head, thinking he maybe preferred Ma all fearful to Ma all defensive, then as Vivian stacked the dishes and scrubbed the table, he filled the basin with hot water and washed the dishes as she dried. He and Ma did the same thing day after day after day. A change was nice.

Joshua woke as Vivian hung the towel to dry.

"I'll get him," Billy said. He liked feeding the baby, and settled in the stuffed chair with Joshua and took the bottle Vivian prepared. Ma studiously kept her head bent over the quilt as Vivian returned to hover by the stove. "Come and sit down," Billy called.

She hesitated. Ma stiffened in protest. "Look, we're all stuck inside. No point in either of you pretending you can't see each other." He ignored the anger boiling in Ma's gaze. "She ain't gonna hurt you." He didn't know if he meant the words for Ma or Vivian. Both needed to hear them.

Vivian edged over to sit in the rocker.

Billy smiled. "Isn't this cozy?" He didn't voice the rest of his thought. If not for the tension between the two women crackling like he suspected the ice on the creek would be doing, this would be kind of nice—a baby in his arms, a woman sitting across from him, Ma at her quilting. The contrast to real life made him laugh silently, mockingly. His hidden chuckle caused his stomach to bounce and Joshua stopped sucking to stare at him with wide-eyed surprise. "Someday you might understand," he murmured to the little one.

Joshua made a happy cooing sound.

Vivian leaned closer. "I think he likes you."

Billy's chest expanded several inches at the idea. And as quickly deflated when Ma snorted. There would be no little babies of his own to hover over. It was a fact of his life. He quickly quenched the wish that things could be different.

Hours later, Ma sighed and finally got up from the stool. Good thing. He was beginning to think she'd never be able to straighten if she didn't leave her position for something else. The only time she looked up was to give Vivian one annoyed look after another as Vivian puttered about the kitchen, mostly moving things from one spot to another and wiping under them. She stomped to the door and shrugged into her coat, stabbed her feet into her boots. "I'm going to give Betsy some extra feed."

A whoof escaped Vivian's lungs as the door closed behind Ma. He knew she'd been as aware of Ma's silent messages as he. She wandered the length of the room, touching pictures on the wall and lifting lamps and other things. She paused at the quilt and bent over to examine it. "This is beautiful. The stitching is an intricate pattern of—" She looked it over more carefully.

"Ma calls it The Garden of Eden."

"I'd like to learn how to do this."

Ma rushed into the room, saw Vivian studying the

quilt and shrieked. Unmindful of her snow-covered boots, she rushed over. "Leave it alone."

Vivian backed up so fast she bumped into the stool. "Sorry. So sorry." She hurried to the rocker and sat down, breathing as if she'd run from the barn in a panic.

Billy fixed Ma with a hard look. Ma gave him an equally hard stare. "She was only looking at it. Admiring it. Said it was beautiful. Any reason that should upset you?"

Ma didn't answer.

Joshua cried to be fed and even though Billy enjoyed holding him, he sensed Vivian's increasing restlessness and let her feed him. And he made up his mind to do something for her. As soon as the baby curled in his bed in peaceful sleep, Billy went into the crowded room where he'd spent the night. Good thing Ma kept everything. In a few minutes, he found a warm coat and boots Pa wore when he was alive. They would be big for Vivian, but warm. He found a woolen cap with earflaps and added it to his pile, which he carried into the other room. "Put these on." He handed the items to Vivian. "I'm going to take you outside."

Ma jerked to her feet. "I'm not looking after the baby."

"We'll be back before he wakes up." He couldn't understand her dislike of Joshua. Ma liked all the other animals. Why not the baby?

Vivian rushed to her feet and pulled on the clothes,

stood dressed and ready before Billy got his own coat on. She almost disappeared in the heavy clothing except for her eyes, which flashed with anticipation. It seemed she looked forward to this as much as he— for entirely different reasons, he reminded himself. He longed to enjoy her company. She wanted to escape Ma's.

She gasped as she stepped outside. "I didn't realize it was this cold."

"It ain't inside."

She laughed. "For which I am grateful."

"You grateful for anything else?" He knew she found Ma a trial.

Vivian turned full circle, her eyes squinting against the bright sun. "For all this beauty," she whispered.

"What do you see?"

"The snow sparkles as if the stars have been poured onto it. The tree branches are iced like a birthday cake."

He liked the way she put words to what he saw. "Do you want to see the animals?"

"I'd love to." Although her eyes crinkled half-shut against the brightness of sun on snow, her face seemed alive with eagerness.

For a moment, he hesitated. Would she find it odd he had such a collection of animals, most of them useless as anything? Or would she see how special they all were?

They stepped into the barn and paused as their eyes adjusted to the muted light. But the cats didn't wait.

They wrapped around his feet. Several of them stood with their front paws on his legs, meowing. Three of them studied Vivian for a moment as if to assess who this stranger was, then decided she would do to rub against.

Billy chuckled. "Meet the rest of the cats."

She looked around, counting. "Eleven?"

He nodded, feeling a tiny bit foolish. To cover it, he whistled and Limpy emerged from the straw pile, shaking himself.

"Oh. Poor dog. What happened to him?"

"Born that way. He's never seemed to mind. Never once heard him complain about missing a leg."

She laughed. "Don't suppose he would."

"When he was younger, he could catch gophers and chase rabbits like any four-legged dog so I guess it hasn't mattered much to him."

Vivian bent and took the dog's chin in her palm. She looked into Limpy's eyes and rubbed behind his ears.

Limpy managed to look as sad and unhappy as any animal could.

"He's faking," Billy said. "Trying to get your sympathy."

"Well, it's working." She patted Limpy's head. "You poor puppy."

Billy snorted. "He hasn't been a puppy for a decade."

"Don't listen to him. I know you're still a puppy at heart."

Billy groaned. The dog was lapping it up like fresh cream. The cats joined the party, pushing against Vivian for attention until she plunked down on the straw-covered floor. She laughed and let the cats crowd to her lap and Limpy push against her shoulder. "They can be very demanding, can't they?"

"They're spoiled rotten. I need to teach them some manners." But he sat on the floor beside her and shared the insistent attention of the animals. After a few minutes, half a dozen of the cats curled into furry balls around Vivian where they began licking their paws and purring.

Vivian laughed. "This is fun. They make me feel so welcome."

Unlike Ma. "Don't pay Ma any mind."

Vivian shrugged. "A little hard not to. Seems like she can't wait to get me out of her house."

"I told you. She's afraid of people." He paused then said the obvious. "And people are afraid of her."

"I remember the stories the kids told at school. About her acting like an Indian. I guess everyone was scared of her."

At least Vivian didn't pretend it wasn't true. "I'm aware of that."

She shifted so she could look him in the face. "Billy, why didn't you keep coming to school? You never gave people a chance to see you're just big, not scary."

Her words eased over his mind like a dose of soothing ointment. He could enjoy this for a long time—

someone to talk to, to share his thoughts with, to enjoy simple pleasures with.

He jerked his thoughts back with cruel decisiveness. In reality, nothing had changed. He was the same, his situation, too. And Vivian would marry Wayne. "I knew they'd never accept me. And for sure, never let Ma forget she'd spent six years living with Indians. As if it was her fault. Pa hoped by moving here she'd get a new start, but everything just followed us. Only it was worse because we were strangers here."

"Maybe if you'd given them more of a chance."

"You mean listen to more nasty things about Ma? I lost Ma for six years. I did nothing to stop the Indians. I wasn't about to pretend I didn't hear what they said."

She tipped her head, her expression troubled. "You blame yourself for the Indians taking her?"

"I hid."

"You were six. You obeyed your mother. Don't you think that's what she wanted? Can you imagine how much worse it would have been for her if you'd been captured, too?"

"She said what kept her going was hoping she'd get back to me."

"There you go."

"I owe her for those years."

She stroked the cats and seemed to consider what to say. "I can understand how you want to protect her. I admire you for that."

As he looked into her eyes, something unfamiliar

made itself known. It reminded him of when he found a wild animal and spent some time gentling it. It was like the first time he knew he'd earned their trust and the animal ate from his hand. Triumph, celebration and connection all rolled up and bound together with joy.

"But now you're both hiding."

His elation died like a bird shot from the sky. "What's wrong with that? If Ma could have hidden like I did, she would not have been captured."

"What are you hiding from now?"

"You've seen Ma. You know what people say about both of us. You think I intend to let people say those things to her face?" He wanted to end this conversation but her gaze held him in a velvet-brown grasp he couldn't escape.

"Perhaps God has something new in store for you."

"Like what?"

"I don't know. Have you ever asked God?"

He searched his mind for a reply. He'd gotten Ma back. He'd always be grateful for that. And he'd found contentment in his life. Finally, he spoke. "I have learned to be content with what I have."

She shook her head. "That doesn't answer my question."

His words didn't satisfy him any more than they did her, but he had no other answer. He never allowed himself to look back, to ask questions for which there were no explanations. Nor did he allow a glance forward. Today was sufficient…until her questions pushed at him. But she didn't know that. Didn't know her questions took him to a place he didn't want to be, couldn't be. He got up. "We better get back." He held out his hand and pulled her to her feet.

Her small hand in his further unsettled his thoughts. He didn't know if he should drop it or continue holding it. He chose the latter without asking himself why.

"I haven't made you angry, have I?"

He tried to untangle his thoughts and decide what he felt. Not anger. Not contentment. Just confusion. "I ain't angry." Though he would almost welcome a good dose of anger. At least he would know what to do with it. A good brisk walk. Or chop a cord of wood. But he didn't like this feeling and had no idea how to handle it.

Vivian sat in front of the fire rocking as if her life depended on it. The trip to the barn with Billy had been a welcome break. But it seemed hours ago. She itched to grab a needle and help Mrs. Black quilt, but the woman made it clear she wouldn't be letting Vivian near her project.

Vivian went over every detail of her only diversion—the visit to the barn. The animals were sweet, obviously well cared for and loved. Seemed the only things that mattered to Billy were his mother and his pets. Too bad. No doubt if he ever let himself care for someone else he would be as loyal, loving and protective as he was with his mother.

A familiar, deep ache pushed at her insides. She wanted exactly what Billy offered his ma. It had been hers when she was a child in Quinten. She hoped to find protection with Wayne. If there was love and affection, so much the better. She hoped there would be. He'd said all the right words when she'd last seen him. But then he'd left and never contacted her.

Time to make supper. Billy enjoyed his meal as always and his ma ate in the pantry but cleaned her plate, so Vivian took that as approval of the food.

Dishes washed and put away, Billy sat before the fire and opened the Bible. "I'm going to read from First Timothy chapter six tonight." He spoke to Vivian then began to read.

She soon understood why he'd chosen this passage.

His deep voice in slow calm tones emphasized each word. "'But godliness with contentment is great gain. For we brought nothing into this world and it is certain we can carry nothing out. And having food and raiment let us be therewith content.'"

He read further but she thought of those words, aching to ask if it meant a person shouldn't want what people gave—friendship, acceptance, companionship? But she would not start such a discussion with his mother in the rocking chair.

Finally, the woman got to her feet and went to her room.

Vivian didn't realize how tense Mrs. Black made her until the door closed behind her and Vivian's shoulders lowered several inches.

Billy remained in the stuffed chair, staring into the fire.

When the baby cried to be fed, Vivian prepared the bottle and sat with the baby in the rocking chair Billy's mother had vacated. Perhaps now she would get a chance to voice her questions.

But it seemed Joshua thought the late evening was his time for attention. Again, he fussed and refused to settle until Billy took him and walked him for a while, singing as he paced. The baby finally quieted.

Billy barely had time to sit down and settle the baby on his chest before Vivian spoke.

"You read that Bible passage on purpose, didn't you?"

"It says what I believe."

"But doesn't it refer to things?" She paused, almost afraid to voice her feelings, knowing they revealed the ache of her heart. Would they trigger similar yearnings for Billy? She couldn't guess if he'd welcome such feelings. He seemed convinced he'd spend the rest of his life with nothing but his ma and his pets. More the pity. He had so much to offer—her cheeks burned as she realized she'd been thinking how he cradled her in his arms, comforted her with a touch... She couldn't remember feeling this way toward Wayne. Had he ever comforted her? Her thoughts seared her with shame.

She intended to marry Wayne and had no call to compare him with another man. "Don't we all need friendship, companionship and acceptance?"

"Is it possible to have them without compromising who we are, perhaps even our moral standards?"

His words sliced through her like she'd swallowed broken glass. "I admit I compromised my standards because of my need for friendship and acceptance."

Chapter Eight

"No. No. I wasn't meaning you and your situation. I meant me. I learned I would have to make such choices if I was to have friends. I would have to pretend my mother didn't exist. I would never do that."

She perceived his invincible integrity and pushed aside her initial reaction of guilt to concentrate on where he intended the conversation to go. "That's very noble. But I'd be lonely."

He sighed deeply, shifting Joshua when he whimpered, and patting his tiny back. "Good thing you don't need to worry about it. You'll soon be back in town."

Yes, back to her goal. A twinge of regret tugged at her thoughts. Regret? No. Billy's gentle presence was comforting only because of Vivian's circumstances—difficult weather and the disappointment of not being able to see Wayne.

"I would have stopped them."

"Pardon?" She had no idea what he meant.

"I would have stopped them from taking you away."

Surprise jolted her limbs. She sat upright so fast the rocker kicked back, almost tossing her from the chair. Not since her parents died had anyone wanted to defend her. Trailing after her surprise came a flush of pleasure. She grinned widely, warmth creeping up her limbs and settling into her chest.

Suddenly, bits and pieces of that day lived in her mind—things she'd completely forgotten until now. "I remember two men and a woman like bats in their long black coats. Mrs. Griswald was one of them. She used to come when Mother had the ladies in for tea. She always wore black and had a ratty old hat with crinkled-up paper flowers on it." She paused, remembering her confusion as these people invaded her house.

"One man kept clearing his throat. It reminded me of a chicken scratching at a piece of wood. Mrs. Griswald stomped ahead of the others and announced in a voice like a summer storm, 'This child is to be removed to a foundling home.' I didn't know it meant orphanage. I didn't know what they wanted. I could barely understand that Mother and Father were gone and not coming back."

Another forgotten memory of that day flooded her mind. "Mr. Styles was there. He said something about the house being sold." Her throat had burned with anger at the words. "I screamed, 'You can't sell our house.' I screamed all sorts of protests. But no one listened. Mrs. Griswald marched me to my room and grabbed a few things. Most of the stuff she picked up and tossed aside. 'You won't be needing this where you're going.' It wasn't until I was on the train I found enough courage to ask when I'd be back. The lady laughed. She said, 'You won't ever be coming back.'" Vivian spouted out the whole story in one breath and stopped to gasp in air. "I didn't know an orphan was nobody. Had no rights. Couldn't even choose where they would live."

"I wish I'd been there."

She imagined him shooing the batlike adults from the house so fast their coats flared into wings.

She looked into his eyes, every heartbeat searing through her like a bolt of lightning. Every breath filled her lungs with a totally unfamiliar storm. The seconds ticked by, counted by the thunder of her pulse. The life-giving blood just below her skin's surface surged with such power it seemed the air vibrated.

And it had absolutely nothing to do with what she wanted in Quinten.

It came from the reassuring gaze of the man across from her.

The baby snuffled and began to fuss.

Vivian blinked and jerked her thoughts back in one sharp movement like snapping a whip. Embarrassed by how much she'd said and how her emotions had veered off path, she couldn't look at Billy. "I'll get a bottle ready."

She offered to take the baby when the milk had warmed but Billy said, "I like feeding the little guy."

Vivian sat across from him again, wishing she had something to occupy her hands—and her mind. She was much too aware of her emotional exposure. But also, she realized with a start, an assurance of being protected, validated, and found worthy. And from such an unlikely source—someone who didn't consider such things necessary.

She sighed. "It isn't as if I haven't done my best since that day."

"I'm sure you did."

She looked at him then. "How would you know that?"

He chuckled. "Because you have a very strong sense of right and wrong. That always includes doing a job well."

"I don't know how you can tell that from what little you've seen of me." She clung to his gaze, something deep inside calling out to him for an answer.

"Vivian Halliday, you rescued your son. You faced a storm to protect him."

She snorted. "We would have both died if you hadn't stumbled on us."

"If God hadn't led me to you."

Again that sense of connection between them. And something else as right and fitting as it was unfamiliar. Vivian couldn't put a name to it. Or rather, she admitted, she circled around the word, afraid of what it meant. Fondness. Caring. Mutual regard. She closed her mind to further examination.

"I see a woman who will always want justice and demand mercy."

His words were a benediction to her soul.

"I thank God He led me to you in the storm." He looked uncomfortable, as if he'd said more than he should, and lowered his gaze to Joshua. "I'm glad I could rescue both of you."

He said no more. But long after Billy had gone to bed, and even after Joshua settled and Vivian lay on the bed in Billy's bedroom, his words surrounded her. She knew she would never forget them. Even after she married Wayne, she'd find comfort in Billy's blessing.

Guilt twisted through her. She shouldn't be thinking of Billy when she planned to marry another.

The next day was even colder. Frost built so thick on the window glass it dimmed the sunlight. Vivian stood before the kitchen window, scratching a peep-hole.

She needed to get to town. Not just for Joshua's sake. For her own. The thoughts she had about Billy had no place in her heart. She'd made one mistake. She wasn't about to make another. But she had nowhere to go until Wayne returned. How long would he be away? Days? Weeks? Heaven forbid, months?

"Have a look in this box." Billy's words pulled her from scratching at the window. "You might find a book you'd like to read."

She hurried to his side. "Thank you." Her eyes over-brimmed with gratitude at his thoughtfulness. It was so like him to think of how to help someone else.

With supreme effort, she jerked her thoughts from heading in that direction, and bent to look through the dozen books. She found one that sounded interesting. Mrs. Black sat at the quilt so Vivian chose the rocking chair and was soon engrossed in the story.

The next day the frost on the window thinned, in-dicating the temperature had moderated.

After breakfast, Billy said, "I'll slip into town and see if Lucas has heard anything, but no point in you and the baby going out."

Mrs. Black gave a strangled shriek then began to mumble.

The skin on Vivian's spine tightened. She avoided looking at Billy, not wanting him to read her fear, which she knew blared brighter than the winter sun. Was she safe alone with Mrs. Black? Would the woman grow more agitated? Even violent? Vivian glanced around. How could she protect herself? Would the broom or poker do any good if the woman went on a demented rage? Her gaze shifted to the baby bed and her heart kicked against her ribs so hard she gasped.

Was the baby in danger? Mrs. Black continued to avoid all contact with Joshua even with Billy's urging.

She stole a look at Mrs. Black, trying to assess her strength. Could Vivian hope to overpower her if she had to?

The woman rocked back and forth mumbling.

Vivian's knees threatened to melt. Mrs. Black hadn't acted so weird since the first afternoon Vivian had invaded her home. Would she get worse when Billy left?

Billy, too, watched his mother, his forehead wrinkled with concern.

Something about Mrs. Black's mumbling caught Vivian's attention. She strained to catch the words.

"Denn Dein ist das Reich und die Kraft und die Herrlichkeit in Ewigkeit."

For thine is the kingdom, and the power, and the glory forever.

The Lord's Prayer in German.

Mrs. Black began again. "Unser Vater im Himmel."

Vivian took a step closer and joined her. "Dein Name werde geheiligt."

Mrs. Black stopped, her mouth working silently as she stared at Vivian. She muttered the next phrase.

Vivian spoke the words with her, never once blinking from the woman's intense look.

Together, they said the entire Lord's Prayer. Silence filled the room when they finished.

"What did you say?" Billy asked, scratching his head and looking curious.

She told him. "The Weimers said it before every meal." Vivian continued to look at Billy's mother, sensing her fragile state. She couldn't tell if the woman intended to retreat further into her past or step into the present, but she knew that she somehow had a say in it by how she handled this moment. She prayed for wisdom from above.

"I pray that all the time," Mrs. Black whispered. "I prayed it when I was with the Indians. It gave me courage. And the Indians feared me. Thought I was—" She circled her finger around her ear. "I pray it still because people think—" Again that circular movement of her finger. "I protect myself with the words."

"Mumbling in a foreign language only convinces them you are—" Vivian tilted her head to indicate the movement Mrs. Black made.

The older woman nodded. "They're afraid of me."

"Yes, they are."

She nodded again. "I'm afraid of them." She began praying in German again.

This time, Vivian accompanied her in English.

Mrs. Black stopped praying and looked confused, perhaps even frightened. Then her expression smoothed, she picked up her needle and returned to quilting.

Vivian's nerves relaxed.

"Well, I'll be," Billy said. He stood uncertainly at the door. "Will you be okay?"

"We'll be okay." The woman wasn't dangerous. Only afraid. And trapped in her fear.

After Billy left, Vivian moved about the room with a sense of freedom. Not that Mrs. Black was suddenly welcoming. She didn't invite Vivian to join her at the quilt, but then neither did she screech and moan. In fact, she seemed quite peaceful.

Until Joshua woke up, loudly demanding his bottle.

Mrs. Black bolted to her feet, sent Vivian an angry look, grabbed her coat and hurried outdoors before Vivian managed to scoop the baby from his bed.

She could only hope the woman would be safe outside. An hour later, Mrs. Black returned and Vivian almost laughed at her relief. Seems she couldn't quite decide what she wanted. She hadn't welcomed being alone with Billy's ma, yet worried when she left and sighed happily when she returned. She'd never known herself to be such a fickle creature.

Vivian waited at the window, watching for Billy's return. The sun hung directly overhead as he rode into the yard and took Blaze to the barn.

"It's so warm the snow is melting," he said, as he stomped into the house. "I 'spect at this rate—"

Vivian couldn't wait for him to finish his weather report. "Was there any news?"

He shook his head. "Lucas says Mrs. Styles was in the store. He asked outright when Wayne would be returning. The woman got all fluttery and said another week at least, then she mumbled something about un-expected news."

Billy tossed his coat and hat at the hook and rubbed his hands together. "A man gets mighty hungry riding to town and back."

Vivian stared at him. He seemed awfully happy for a man who just learned he was stuck with an uninvited guest for at least another week. She glanced at him. He avoided looking directly at her then slowly, he stilled his restless hands, swallowed hard and met her gaze, his eyes bright with meaning. She shied away, afraid of what she glimpsed, afraid of what he might see in her face, even more afraid of what she felt.

It was wrong to be relieved she had this respite, a few more days to enjoy the way Billy made her feel.

She hurried to the stove and dished up the food. "I made dinner. Expected you would be hungry when you got back."

"You can count on that." He parked himself and waited for Vivian to join him. He glanced at his ma, questioning her with a lift of his eyebrows.

Vivian held her breath as the woman hesitated, glanced at the empty chair, sent Vivian a considering look as if wondering if she was enemy or not, then slowly got to her feet and shuffled toward the table. Halfway across the room she paused, gave a desperate look in the direction of the pantry, then mumbled something Vivian thought was "deliver us from evil" in German and continued toward the table.

Vivian ducked her head as she smiled. Mrs. Black would soon learn Vivian meant evil toward no one.

Billy patted his ma's hand when she sat in the chair. "Let's pray." He bowed his head and for a moment, was silent. "Thank you, God, for happy hearts, for snow and sunny weather. Thank you, God, for this food and that we are together. Amen."

Vivian kept her head bowed for a second after Billy finished. She knew his gratitude was meant for his mother, yet it felt good to be included in *together* if only because she sat at the same table.

Billy hunched over his meal. Although he wasn't about to admit it to anyone, and didn't much care for having to admit it himself, he'd been glad when Lucas said Wayne would be gone longer. It meant Vivian and the baby stayed longer. He'd get to hold the little guy, settle him at night. Maybe he could show Vivian some of his favorite places—the path by the creek, the place where violets grew every spring. She might never see them, but he could tell her what it was like though it wasn't the same as sharing the event would be.

He slammed a fist into his thoughts.

He needed nobody. Managed just fine by himself, thank you one and all.

But holding that tiny little critter and having him smile up at him was about the greatest pleasure he'd known in some time. Except for one thing—Vivian's company.

Last night, sitting by the fire with her, listening to her story, he'd struggled to stop himself from cradling her to his chest like he did little Joshua. No one had the right to treat another the way those people had treated Vivian simply because she was small and helpless. If he'd been there, he would have fought for her. Even now, he'd do all he could to protect and help her.

He groaned silently.

The best way he could help her would be to see her and Wayne reunited and see that she and Joshua got the happy family he wished for.

Again he stifled a groan. What was he thinking? He had a family. He and Ma.

He concentrated on his food. He intended to keep his head squarely parked on his shoulders, but allowed himself one quick glance at Vivian.

She chased her food around the plate with no sign of giving it a lift to her mouth. She sighed. That sound was about more'n he could stand.

Again that ache in his arms as he fought the desire to wrap her to his chest and shelter her from distress.

He wanted to ease the worry filling her eyes with such darkness. "I'll go back to town in a few days and see if there is further news."

"Oh, but—" She shifted her gaze back to him and paused to suck in air. "I appreciate your help."

He couldn't stop his grin from widening, stretching his cheeks to their limit. "Don't mind at all."

Ma slammed her fork to the table. "Foolishness."

Billy only laughed. "Ma, I'd help an animal in trouble. Guess I can bend myself to help a human."

They finished the meal and he began to wash dishes, a job he'd despised until a few days ago. Now he eagerly dipped his hands into the soapy water. And he wasn't blind as to why he suddenly enjoyed the task. It gave him a chance to have Vivian at his side. He didn't have to move much to wash the stack of dishes, which saved him the possibility of crashing into anything. She fluttered from table to stove to the cupboards as quick and graceful as a deer he'd watched playing in a grassy clearing one day. It pleasured him considerably to have her twirl by him as she worked. Sort of gave him a solid feeling.

She brushed his arm as she reached for a dish.

Every bone in his body felt ready to melt like warm butter. If he moved, he'd surely stagger. Maybe into Vivian. His size often made him feel clumsy, but he'd never before had his body act like it had a mind of its own—wanting to reach for her to steady her as she spun past despite his intention of remaining indifferent. His heartbeat drummed in his ears. He needed air. He told his chest muscles to work. *Breathe, man.* With a noisy rush he filled his lungs, sucking in air until he could again feel his toes.

Vivian looked at him. "I know you're helping me out of the goodness of your heart."

The way she said it washed his insides with warm

honey. As if she might look up to him. He grinned mockingly—everyone looked up to him. He ducked his head for fear she'd think he laughed at her. But to know her approval, well, if Ma measured his chest size right now she'd find it at least four inches bigger than usual.

Vivian paused at his side, wiping a pot. "I want you to know how much I appreciate it."

"Glad to help out." Glad to bring a smile to her lips and happiness to her life if only for a minute or two. Why, he'd walk through— And why was he thinking such foolish things? She'd go to town and her life with Wayne and he'd stay here with his ma and his life. Chances were they'd never see each other again once this little episode ended.

The plain, blunt, inescapable truth was he didn't want it to end.

He had to stop thinking along those lines.

Chapter Nine

He grabbed for something to talk about. Something that didn't remind him Vivian would leave as soon as Wayne returned. "Tell me about your friend at the orphanage." He scrubbed a pot with excess vigor.

"Marie?"

He nodded as if he had forgotten her friend's name but he remembered everything she'd told him. Down to the way her eyes looked and her mouth moved when she'd given him the information.

"She's twenty—a year older than me." Vivian laughed softly. "If not for Marie, I might have turned into a self-pitying, overly defensive person. She saw how hurt I was by what happened. And how frightened. I'd been pampered as a child. I didn't know how to do all the chores expected of me and I knew nothing about babies." She chuckled again. "I guess you must have seen how little I still know about babies."

He nodded, feeling his grin all the way to the corners of his heart. "Made me mighty suspicious."

"Marie taught me how to do my assigned chores, but more than that, she told me how to handle life. I didn't buy all her philosophies but she certainly turned me in the right direction when she said, 'You don't get a say in what happens to you, but no one can tell you how to feel or act or dream. Do your work, but keep your dreams.'" Vivian looked thoughtful. "Thanks to her, I did exactly that. Maybe too well. I agreed to everything I was told to do. Never allowed myself dreams, though."

"What about now? Any dreams?"

She paused, looked far away, thoughtful, her expression a little regretful. "My dream is to give Joshua the kind of home I had as a child. I want him to be loved and cherished."

Joshua started to squall.

She laughed. "He must know I'm talking about him." She put the last pot away, hung the towel and prepared the bottle before she went to get him. Angry at being made to wait, Joshua screamed.

"Hush, now. You're not going to starve," Vivian murmured.

Billy watched Vivian, her face glowing with love for her son. But he felt a tremor of sadness. Her only dream was for Joshua. Mighty noble. But didn't she have any dreams of her own?

* * *

That evening, Joshua set up his usual fuss and calmed only when Billy took him and walked him. After a while, Billy decided Joshua had settled enough to allow him to take advantage of a chair. Still bouncing the baby and humming, he sat across from Vivian. He looked forward to this evening time—a chance to hold little Joshua and visit with Vivian. He ignored how foolish it was in light of how soon it would be a thing of the past.

Vivian leaned back as if she enjoyed this quiet time together as much as he. "What did you and your father do while your mother was gone?"

"Pa's sister stayed with us a while, but then she found some lucky farmer to marry and left. We had a few other women come. I can hardly remember them so I guess they didn't stay long. Finally, Pa said we'd manage as best we could on our own. I soon learned to sweep the floor and do dishes and we cooked simple-enough meals. I weren't fussy so long as I got enough. Pa knew that better'n any of the women he'd hired. Seems they thought I should eat dainty meals. Did I ever start to grow when Pa let me eat as much as I needed." He chuckled, remembering the growth spurt he took. "I was twelve when Ma came back and she couldn't believe how big I was. Taller than her and I outweighed her considerably." He closed his eyes as he recalled the day the sheriff escorted her home. "She was thin as a straw." He shut his mind to remembering but couldn't stop the wayward direction of his thoughts. Ma so afraid. Acting so strange. Not at all like the Ma he remembered.

"Billy, I feel bad for both of you. Your poor ma must have suffered something awful and you must have missed her so much. And then she came back but she was—"

He opened his eyes and held her gaze in a hard look. "She ain't crazy."

"I know that." She gave him hard look for hard look. "But doesn't it seem she's stuck in her past?"

Her unspoken accusation he was somehow at fault annoyed him. "You don't know nothing about her. Besides, why does it matter to you?"

She ducked her head. "I'm sorry. I know it's none of my business."

He wanted to pull his words back, return the sense of connection they'd been sharing.

Slowly, she lifted her head, her brown eyes warm with compassion. "Don't you have any dreams?"

The words crashed through him, rolling like thunder into the far corners of his heart, reverberating across his thoughts like fingers over a scrub board. He had dreams. And sitting across from her, sharing time with her, seeing the dark stillness of her eyes, holding her tiny son, gave those dreams lightning-clear form. Inside him glowed a tender feeling that could easily grow into love if he wasn't careful. He tamped down his yearnings, bolted the door on his reaction. She would wed another. He would remain here with his mother. His dreams could not be acknowledged.

She waited, her eyes wide as if she'd seen a hint of his struggle.

"I got all I need right here. My ma. My pets. The great outdoors and God up in heaven."

She nodded slowly but her expression said she didn't accept it.

He hoped she would not pursue the topic. He had enough difficulty convincing himself without trying to convince her.

They settled into an uneasy pattern over the next days. Ma seemed to have accepted the presence of Vivian and the baby. She wasn't particularly welcoming but at least she was settled, spending quiet hours working at her quilt and joining them at the table for meals.

Billy had no complaints. Not about the food— Vivian continued to make meals that were not only filling but delicious. Most of all, he looked forward to the quiet evenings. He anticipated them far too much. Every day Vivian and the baby stayed increased his longing for more than he could have.

A few days later, the sun shone with such warmth he opened the barn door so all the animals could go outdoors. The frost melted from the windows of the house. He finished the chores, spent time with the animals, giving them extra attention, trying to stay away from the house. Eventually, he ran out of busy work and leaned against the fence. He hadn't had a walk since Vivian and the baby came. Had the snow changed the shape of things? Done any damage to the trees along the creek? He wanted to see.

His breath escaped in an explosive sound. He wanted to show Vivian all his special places before she left. He gripped the board under his fingers as if holding on to the wood could enable him to hold on to his feelings. But his desire to share his pleasures, just this once, grew. He groaned. He was a strong man. Surely, he could control his emotions.

The sun warmed his face. It was a perfect day. They'd be able to see for miles. And he could just imagine the light on the ice.

One day. What would it hurt?

He headed for the house.

Vivian stood in the doorway, her gaze drifting into the distance as if she felt as restless as he.

Suddenly, his insides warmed and he didn't feel guilty. He was doing this for her. "Grab the baby. We're going for a walk."

She blinked as she realized what he said, then eagerness flooded her face. "I'd like that." She hurried to wrap Joshua in blankets.

Ma had shifted her chair so she worked in the sunlight. She shot him a hard look.

He wanted to assure her it was just a walk even though in the farthest corner of his heart, beyond reason and reality, lay a tender feeling, a sweet regard that he knew would look a lot like love if he examined it.

He had no intention of doing so.

Today, he would simply enjoy the sunshine and Vivian's company.

Within minutes, both Vivian and the baby were ready. "Where are we going?"

"To the creek." There was more to see. Lots more. But they'd turn back at the creek. He took the baby and shortened his step so Vivian could easily keep up. He liked having her at his side.

She lifted her face to the sun and laughed. "Such a nice day."

"Yup." Perfect in every way imaginable. If he could forever keep one day, this would be the one he'd pick. He paused as they passed the buildings and the open prairie lay before them. "Every spring, I see hundreds of antelope cross here. They're so curious, they will follow me at a safe distance. If something spooks them, they run off. I've heard they can outrun many a horse."

"Really?"

"Yup." When had that become his favorite word? He told her everything he knew about antelope though he couldn't imagine she cared. But her eyes sparkled as if the whole topic held incredible interest, so he rambled on.

They reached a little knoll and he turned her toward the open plain. Snowdrifts rippled across the prairie, creating black shadows in contrast to the brilliant light cast by the sun.

She sighed. "It's beautiful."

"In the summer, silver sagebrush dots the land. But for real beauty, you should see it on a moonlit night. It's all silvery white. So lonely and so peaceful. And in the spring, purple and yellow flowers patch it like one of Ma's crazy quilts. And in the fall, the leaves of those low bushes turn a deep red."

"I'd love to see it."

He stilled the ache squeezing up his throat, and shifted Joshua in his arms as if by so doing he could stop his thoughts from their wayward trek. How he'd love to show her this scene in every season.

"Maybe I can come back and visit when spring comes." She sounded wistful. They both knew once she married, there was little chance of her returning.

They stood a bit longer, drinking in the scene. Billy filled his mind with strength and determination born of the vastness before him. "Let's see the creek." But once he turned away, his weakness returned. He shifted Joshua so he could take Vivian's elbow as if she needed help navigating the trail when it was, in truth, not difficult. He welcomed the few drifts requiring his assistance.

They walked in companionable silence until they approached the streambed. Snow had drifted around the trees lining the bank. "Wait while I break a path." He handed her the baby and stomped a trail through the snow. And he tried not to think of the things he wanted and couldn't have, all wrapped up in a black woolen coat, watching as he flattened the snow. She was backlit by the bright sunlight, her face full of enjoyment, the baby in her arms peeking from his blanket.

He reached the other side of the drift. The creek lay before him, patches of blue ice swept to a polish, broken by fingers of snow scratching across the surface.

"It's so peaceful."

He'd heard her approach, but forced himself not to turn when every muscle of his body bunched up wanting to open his arms and welcome her into an embrace. "It is peaceful."

"Do you come here often?"

How often was often? "I come when I want to think or pray. In the summer, I sit over there and watch the water ripple by."

"What do you watch in the winter?"

He smiled. He might be able to show her. "You want to sit down?" He whipped off his coat and put it on a spot where the grass had blown clear.

"You'll freeze."

"I'm tough."

She considered the coat, took in his heavy shirt, lifted her gaze to his eyes and studied him.

Feeling a little goofy because of how much he wanted to share some time with her, maybe doing nothing but staring at the frozen creek, he grinned. "Colder standing than sitting, I 'spect."

"Very well." She sat on one end of his coat.

He sat, too. Had to sit pretty close in order to share the fabric. Didn't mind a bit that it provided an excuse to touch shoulders with her. He noted with heart-swelling satisfaction that she made no move to shift away.

"This is nice."

He didn't care if she meant the scene, or the peacefulness. He pretended she meant sitting close to him. His mind flooded with things he wanted to say to her. But he had no right, and the words iced into great immovable blocks.

She looked to one side and gasped. "Look." She touched the back of his hand, sent a jolt to his heart.

He swallowed hard and followed the direction she indicated. A big buck deer tiptoed from the trees and picked his way to the creek. He appeared to examine it for a place not frozen, found a spot where snow had melted on top of the ice and daintily lapped at the water. He lifted his head, glanced about then drank some more.

Joshua gurgled happily.

The buck bounced away, gone as silently as it came.

Vivian's hand rested on Billy's arm. "That's one of the nicest things I've ever seen."

He studied her hand, amazed that such a small slim

thing could cause such heaviness in his lungs, making it difficult to pull in a satisfying breath.

He forced his gaze away. A long sigh eased over his lips. "I guess we should head back before this little guy demands to be fed again." He scrambled to his feet and reached down to pull her up.

They stood facing each other. He feared all he tried not to feel pooled in his eyes, like the little bit of melted water pooling in the low spot on the river. He wished—

"Thank you," she murmured. She rested her hands on his crossed arms. "You're really a very good man. You should give people a chance to discover it." She stretched up on tiptoe and kissed his cold, whisker-roughed chin.

As she realized her boldness, heat flooded Vivian's cheeks and threatened to melt her borrowed coat off her shoulders. She hurried across the snowy path.

"You're welcome." He sounded as surprised as she was by her action.

She didn't hear his footsteps and turned.

He stared after her, his fingers pressed to the spot she had kissed. He looked as though she had shaken him to his toes.

A slow satisfaction warmed her. "Are you coming?"

He grabbed up his coat and tramped after her.

"I think he realizes what he's missing stuck out here," she whispered to Joshua before Billy caught up. Her satisfaction fell out the bottom of her heart. She would be missing something, too, when she left—a chance to see all the beauties he talked about, a chance to share more of these special times.

But she would be with Wayne. And she'd easily forget this pause in her life. After all, she must have felt just as pleased to spend time with Wayne or she wouldn't be in this situation.

But to her distress, she couldn't remember having this wonderful, scary sense of shared awe.

That evening, after Mrs. Black retired and Vivian and Billy sat around the fire with Joshua on Billy's chest, Vivian brought up something that had been bothering her.

"Billy, how long are you and your ma going to hide here?"

He did his best to reveal no surprise at her question but she'd seen the little jerk that made Joshua protest. "We ain't hiding. Everyone knows where we live."

"You know what I mean. You hole up here like there is no outside world."

"I been to town twice in the last week."

"On my behalf. I thank you for that. But when do you go for yourself?"

"Nothing in town I want." His voice grew more and more harsh.

"What about your ma? Wouldn't she enjoy visiting with friends once she got over her nervousness?"

"She's got no friends in town."

Vivian remembered something she'd heard so long

ago she couldn't recall who'd said it. "Strangers are just friends we haven't met yet."

Billy snorted, quietly, careful not to disturb Joshua. "Or could be they're just people who'd be unkind if you gave them a chance."

"Not everyone is cut from the same cloth." She was concerned about his mother stuck out here without friends or a social life but she didn't mean for him to consider his options solely for his mother's sake. "You're a nice man. You should go out and meet others. Maybe some day you'll find a nice woman and get married." Something wrenched inside her at the thought. Something selfish and inappropriate considering she had a child by another man, and intended to make things right by marrying the other man. *Lord, send Wayne home soon before I lose my way again.* Not that she'd allow herself the same sin but she was dangerously close to falling in love with Billy.

And that just couldn't happen.

"That ain't possible, now is it? You see how Ma is afraid of strangers. And I could never force her to do something that would make her so unsettled."

A million arguments raced through Vivian's head as she considered his look that seemed as full of regret as her own heart.

She wanted to say it was time to push Ma into society. Surely, she would adjust. She wanted to tell him some things were worth upsetting the calm routine they had become slaves to. She wanted…

None of the things she wanted were possible and what Billy and his ma did was none of her business.

She had to keep her goal in mind. Had to accept responsibility for her sin and do what she could to make it right. But a wide beam of pain ploughed through her thoughts and bludgeoned her heart. If only she hadn't sinned. If only she'd paid heed to what she knew was right. Now she must bear the price.

But she would not make Joshua pay a similar price.

Lord, I'm so sorry. I'll do my best to do what is right from now on. Just send Wayne back so he can give Joshua the honor of his name.

There was so much she wanted to say to Billy. Like how he had no reason to hide. Nor did his ma. They were decent people.

Like how she'd miss him and wished she'd glimpse him in town. Ahh. She mentally protested the pain that had not passed. How could she be such a wanton, wayward woman? A child by a man she hadn't married and aching for yet another man. Guilt and shame at her thoughts, her yearnings, her weaknesses, rolled through her like a giant wave.

"Something the matter?" Billy asked.

She could not let him guess at what bothered her. "Sometimes I am so full of self-loathing at the mistakes I've made." She might as well call a sin a sin. "I've sinned against God, and Joshua will bear the price unless I marry Wayne." She didn't mean it the

way it came out. As if she didn't want to marry Wayne.
As if the idea meant sacrifice.

To think so made her sin seem even worse. It was
one thing to make a baby with a man she loved and
hoped to marry. It was quite another to make one with
a man who had done nothing more than offer her
kindness.

But he'd done more. He still would. She just needed
to see him and things would fall into order.

The look in Billy's eyes was gentle and she clung
to it. Apart from Marie's support, she'd seen nothing
but accusation and condemnation in the eyes of those
around her since it became obvious she was with child.

"Vivian, there is a story in the Bible that I think you
need to remember. It's the story of a woman caught in
sin. A sin similar to what you refer to. Men dragged
her before the Lord with the intention of stoning her
to death. Do you remember the story?"

She shook her head.

He pulled down his Bible. "I think it's in John
chapter eight." He turned the fragile pages. "Yes, here
it is." He began to read about a woman caught in
adultery.

Vivian hadn't been caught in the act of immorality
but there was no way to hide the fact she'd participated
in it. Joshua was evidence. Poor baby. What she'd done
to him was so awful.

Billy continued to read. "Now hear what Jesus said.
'He that is without sin among you, let him first cast a

stone at her.' Then down a bit further, 'Neither do I condemn thee; go, and sin no more.'" He closed the Bible.

She'd never heard that story before. She'd heard the ten commandments. She'd heard all sorts of warnings about sin and be sure your sin will find you out. She had no reason to doubt that. Nor would Joshua. Her innocent little son would be marked by her sin. Tears flowed unchecked down her cheeks.

Billy shifted the baby and leaned forward to brush them from her face. "Vivian, none of us has the right to judge unless we are free of sin and none of us are. Jesus alone is sinless and what does he say? 'Neither do I condemn thee.'"

She shook her head back and forth, unable to speak, unable to believe the words.

"That's what the Bible says," he insisted.

"But it can't be true."

He smiled. "Why not?"

"Because that's not how it is. Having a baby out of wedlock is a great sin."

A dark expression crossed his face. "Maybe what you mean is that people judge some sins more harshly and this is one of them. Maybe because it can't be hidden."

"I don't want to hide Joshua. He deserves a normal life."

His expression grew almost harsh. "Then you must do what is necessary to give him that."

"Yes."

He sat back.

She felt his withdrawal in a more real sense than just the way he put physical distance between them. She saw it in his face and in the coolness in the air that made her shiver.

They both knew what she must do.

For Joshua's sake.

The coolness between them remained the next day. It confused her. Had she offended him by suggesting he should try and get his ma to visit town? Or had her talk about wanting a normal life for Joshua reminded him of the lack in his own life even though he insisted he was quite happy with nothing but the farm and his pets and no one but his ma?

After lunch, Billy jumped to his feet. "Someone is coming."

Mrs. Black shrieked and headed for the pantry. "Make them go away," she called.

"Ma, it's only the young Malone lad. You remember the Malones. They run the bakery next to Lucas's store."

Mrs. Black moaned but Vivian sprang to the window. Was the boy delivering the message she hoped for? And dreaded. Once Wayne returned, she would have to confront the harsh reality of her sin and throw herself at Wayne's mercy. He would have no choice but to marry her. She had no choice but to accept his marriage.

For Joshua's sake. For Joshua's sake.

And once she saw Wayne again, her feelings for him would return. He'd kiss her as he had in the past and all her uncertainty would vanish.

Billy strode out to meet the boy and nodded a couple of times then returned to the house as the boy reined his horse around and headed back to town.

Vivian couldn't breathe as she waited for him to relay the news.

"Lucas says Wayne is to return on the train tomorrow." Billy's voice was strangely expressionless.

"Tomorrow?" She took a step toward the baby sleeping in his little bed. Stopped. Turned back to look out the window. "I—" She tried to think what to do.

"The train arrives early in the day. I'll take you toward noon."

She nodded. *Calm down. This is what you came for.*

But her insides seemed to have been sucked clean, leaving nothing but an empty, scared feeling.

As if sensing her emotions, Billy patted her shoulder. "This time tomorrow things will be all sorted out."

That's right. Tomorrow. But she couldn't seem to pull her thoughts that far ahead. Tonight would be her last night shared with Billy.

Now why that should make her sad was inexcusable. By this time tomorrow, she would be making plans to marry Wayne. That's why she was here.

She strode over to pluck Joshua from the bed and pressed him to her chest. Her first and only consideration was doing what was best for him.

That night, Billy seemed as strained as she as they sat by the fire. This was the last time they'd do this. Vivian sucked in a deep breath. Maybe she and Wayne could do something similar. She tried to comfort herself with the thought.

Billy sighed—a long, lonesome sound that trembled over her own nervousness, setting her muscles to twitching.

"I'm gonna miss the little guy." He pulled the Bible from the shelf. "I want to read you something." He turned pages until he found what he wanted. "Psalms twenty-nine, verse eleven, 'The Lord will give strength to his people; the Lord will bless his people with peace.'" He closed the Bible. "God's promise to you. My prayer for you."

Her throat tightened but she managed to speak calmly. "Thank you. I wish I had my own Bible. My parents had one but it disappeared along with everything else. The Weimers had a Bible but it was in German. I wouldn't have understood it even if I'd been allowed to read it."

But Billy's words would provide comfort in the days ahead.

Chapter Ten

For the first time in his life, Billy wished for a blinding snow storm. A three-day blow that would make travel impossible. He mumbled to himself as he hitched Blaze to the wagon. He was a man of simple wants. He accepted what life handed him and made the best of it. He did not build impossible dreams.

Limpy whimpered.

Billy patted the dog's head. "Not to worry, old friend. I ain't lost my mind." Though if anyone could read his thoughts they might have cause to wonder.

Absently, he scratched behind Limpy's ears and petted the cats. Yeah, he'd miss Vivian and Joshua. But he didn't regret what must be done. He'd spent far too many years as a social outcast. He'd do everything in his power to see that Vivian and Joshua didn't suffer the same fate. That meant seeing them safely into town and wishing them the very best in a life with Wayne.

"That's the way things have to be," he told his faithful pets. "At least you'll all be here when I get back."

He led Blaze and the wagon to the step and went to the door.

Vivian sat in the rocker holding Joshua. Her few belongings sat by the door awaiting their departure.

He expected she might be both nervous and excited. Instead, she looked like the sun had flown from her sky. Her eyes looked straight through him, wide as a deer's just before it dashed away after being startled by a sudden sound. Only Vivian showed no sign of moving. His heart went out to her. What she was about to do wasn't easy.

Ma sat at her quilt, her head down, but Billy saw she watched Vivian out of the corner of her eye and he wondered what she thought. Would she be glad to have the pair gone? Would she ever be willing to face the public?

He dismissed the thought. It was only Vivian's questioning that brought it to mind. He'd tried so often to get Ma to change. Every time had been disastrous until he finally accepted she either couldn't or wouldn't ever change. And he couldn't abandon her.

He shifted his attention back to Vivian. Wondered if she suddenly wished she could hide here, too. Just like Ma. But life had too much to offer her and Joshua. He moved to her side and touched her shoulder. "Vivian, it's time to leave."

She blinked three times and thrust out a sigh. "I'm

ready." She took the hand he offered and let him pull her to her feet. "I'm ready." He knew this time she meant she was ready to deal with her future.

He loaded them in the wagon, thankful the weather made travel more pleasant than the last time he'd taken her to town.

He parked himself on the seat beside her.

Joshua peeked out from his covers.

Billy touched his nose. "You have no idea of what lays ahead, do you, young man?" He was going to meet his father for the first time and start a new life as the youngest Mr. Styles. How long would it take for Wayne and Vivian to marry?

The sun stung his eyes and he scrubbed them with the heel of his hand so he could see better.

He wouldn't think of how much he would miss Vivian's sweet presence, and the joy of feeding and rocking Joshua. He'd think only of how they'd be so well taken care of and accepted, how they would find their place in the social life of town.

They reached the bottom of the lane. "Would you mind stopping a moment?"

He did so, wondering what she wanted.

She turned to look back at the farm. She laid splayed fingers to her chest and seemed to stop breathing. Then she nodded, turned her gaze to him, her brown eyes revealing acceptance and determination. "Thank you."

There was little to say as they continued the journey. Several times she lifted her face to the sky, her eyes closed, the sun tracing feathery outlines of her lashes against her cheeks.

He thought she was praying and added his silent petition. *Lord, God, she is doing what is right and noble. Bless her. Give her courage to face this challenge and most of all, give her and the little one a happy life.*

Praying restored his peace of mind and purpose, and tension dropped from his shoulders.

They approached town. The familiar reluctance caught at his hands and he squeezed the reins. He had no desire to encounter the stares and whispers of the good, righteous townspeople so he again sought out the back route to the bank.

They reached their destination. But neither of them moved. Each, he supposed, for their own reasons. She, no doubt, a little afraid. He, reluctant for this final step.

He didn't know if she wanted him to keep Joshua again, like last time, while she made arrangements to meet Wayne in private.

As they hesitated, a man with a broad, shiny face tromped down the sidewalk leading from the front of the bank to the alley.

"I'll ask him if Wayne is in." He called to the man and asked the question.

The man answered with much arm waving and an accent so deep that Billy understood a fraction of what he said. He thanked the man and waited until he was out of hearing. "Did you get that?"

"I think he said Wayne was not at the bank."

At least they both understood that much. "Did he say Wayne was at his house?"

"I think so."

"Then I suppose it's best I take you there."

She pulled Joshua closer and nodded.

The Styleses lived at the south end of town. Meant he had to cross several streets. He avoided the main street as he made his way to the big fine house. He'd never been inside but the house had three stories, four dormer windows on the second story and on the main level, a big bay window facing the street. From the back where he stopped the wagon, there was a large, glassed-in porch, more dormer windows and a variety of outbuildings. The house was always painted. In the summer, the yard was always perfectly groomed. Not by either of the Mr. Styleses, though. They had a gardener. And a cook. Would they allow Vivian to enjoy preparing any of the food?

"We're here."

"Yes."

"I suspect you ought to go to the front door."

"I'll walk around." The house was on a corner lot.

He finally forced himself from the seat to help her down. He shifted his hands to her arms. "I hope things work out well for you and little Joshua."

"You've been a wonderful help. Perhaps I'll see you about town?"

"Could happen." She smiled up at him, her eyes round with so many emotions he couldn't begin to name them but knowing her nervousness made it impossible to let her go. "You'll do just fine."

"Thank you. For everything." She picked up the basket that held Joshua's things.

He dropped his hands to his side and stepped back. He wished he could see her safely inside but it wouldn't do her cause any good to be seen in his company. "Goodbye."

She nodded, tore her gaze from his and stared at the house. She shivered once, then lifted her head. "Goodbye and thank your ma for allowing me to stay."

He chuckled. "I'll be sure to do that."

She smiled, allowing her lungs to do their job. She'd be fine. After all, she'd faced far harder things than going to a man who must surely love her seeing as he'd given her a baby.

She headed down the sidewalk.

He waited until she turned the corner before he climbed back into the wagon and drove away. He did not look back as he returned the way he had come and pulled up behind the general store and went inside to get the papers Lucas would have for him and the thread Ma wanted.

Lucas joined him in the back room. "Where's Vivian and the baby? They still with you?"

"I left them at the Styles house."

"Then you haven't heard?"

Billy's scalp tightened at the sound in Lucas's voice.

"Wayne came back with a wife."

Vivian didn't let her steps slow until she reached the front door. She put the basket down, adjusted Joshua in her arms so he faced outward, ready to smile at Wayne. She patted her hair and glanced down at her cape. She'd brushed it so it was clean enough. For the first time in days, she thought of the plainness of her dress and wished she had something nicer, but Wayne had paid court to her when she wore a dress no different than this one. He hadn't seemed to mind then. No reason why he should now.

She straightened her shoulders and prayed for God's hand of mercy on her. Not that she deserved it, but for Joshua's sake. She recalled the words Billy had read from the Bible. *Neither do I condemn thee.* Hardly seemed possible, but all that mattered for her right now was getting this meeting over with. She grabbed the brass knocker and clanged it.

She heard a voice call within and steps heading for the door and she held Joshua closer.

The door handle rattled.

Her heart clung to her throat.

The door opened. And Wayne stood as handsome as she remembered, his brown hair combed back in a perfect wave. He wore a fine, brown wool suit.

"Wayne," she whispered.

"Vivian." He stepped out and pulled the door closed behind him. "What are you doing here?"

He didn't sound welcoming. Though, of course, he was likely surprised to see her. But hadn't he said he would never forget her?

"Aren't you happy to see me?"

"No." His glance darted to Joshua.

She pulled herself taller. "Wayne, say hello to your son."

He made a noise full of harsh disbelief. "I take it he's your little illegitimate child. He's certainly not my son."

Her insides iced over at his harsh, condemning words. "Well, he is. If you recall your visit to the Weimers' almost a year ago, you might also recall how you took me out, how we…how you…"

"Dear?" Someone pulled the door open.

Vivian expected it would be Mrs. Styles wondering who had come to the door, but the woman who slipped out and took Wayne's arm in a most possessive way was young and pretty and wearing a gown that looked like it had been cut from a fashion magazine.

Wayne smiled at the woman. Much like the smile Vivian remembered he once favored her with. He faced Vivian, his smile still in place but his eyes cold.

She shivered at his look.

"It's just someone with a business question." He

pulled the woman close. "May I present my wife, Isabelle Styles."

Everything inside Vivian died. She stammered something she hoped resembled a reasonable greeting.

"We have no more business to discuss." Wayne backed away and shut the door in Vivian's face.

She stood rooted to the spot. This was not how it was to be. Wayne was Joshua's father. As such, he was to marry Vivian and give his son a name. And a home.

What would she do now?

Billy stared at Lucas, unable to accept the news he'd heard. "What did you say?"

"He's married. Came back with a wife. A pretty young thing, everyone says."

"But I left Vivian there." He knew Lucas understood the reason.

"I don't imagine she'll be welcomed."

Alarm skidded through Billy's body, nailed him to the floor. Vivian would be shocked. She'd have no place to go. What would she do? "I've got to find her." He bolted for the door, leaped to the wagon and slapped the reins.

The fastest way was straight down the main street and he headed in that direction, the wagon box bouncing in the frozen ruts, Blaze leaning into the harness as he responded to Billy's wild yell. Billy saw startled faces as he flashed past. A rider jerked back on his reins to avoid a collision and the rider hollered for him to slow down. He yelled a warning to another wagon to get out of the way and skidded around the corner as he turned toward the Styleses' house. He paid no heed to his own safety and only a fleeting thought for those he passed. Vivian would be lost, alone, no place to go. He had to find her.

He cranked on the reins and rattled to a halt in front of the Styleses' house. The door was closed. The house silent. A flicker of a curtain in one window and then nothing. He glanced every direction. No sign of Vivian. Had they invited her inside? Decided to be civilized about this?

Only one way to find out.

He tied the reins, murmured to Blaze to wait and ran to the door, though anyone watching would likely call it a lumbering gait. He'd never been graceful running. Too big for that.

He took the three steps as one, rattled the knocker. Rattled it again then pounded.

Wayne jerked the door back, shielding himself with the solid slab of wood. "Would you stop that?"

Billy had never cared for this man. He was a bully. Whenever he chose to mock Billy as a child, he always made sure he was surrounded by friends or could easily escape to the protection of a teacher or other authority figure. Not that Billy would beat the man. He didn't care for violence.

Except for that one time. He'd come upon Wayne kicking a kid he accused of stealing a coin he'd dropped. Billy had stopped the abuse. Oh, he hadn't hit the man, though he was sorely tempted. He'd simply caught Wayne's fist and squeezed it until Wayne practically cried and forgot all about the defenseless child, which was all Billy cared about.

Wayne had been angry since that day. It was four years ago so he guessed Wayne wasn't the forgiving sort.

"Is she here?"

Wayne snorted. "That depends on who you are asking about."

"You know who I mean. Vivian. Is she here?"

"Why would she be here? Despite anything she might have told you, she's nothing to me. Nor is her little illegitimate child."

Billy's fist bunched. He took a step forward. "Why you…"

Wayne shoved the door toward him, his face white with fear.

Billy stuck his boot against the frame to stop the door from closing. "She deserves better than you, anyway." He turned and jumped off the step.

Brave little Wayne opened the door and followed him as far as the top step. "You are quite right. She deserves someone like you."

Billy growled low in his throat and turned to face the man but Wayne stepped back.

"Tell her I don't want to see her again. I got what I wanted a year ago."

Billy roared and leaped up the steps.

"And I don't mean the baby." Wayne slammed the door.

Billy steamed toward the wagon and climbed to the seat. He sat with the reins dangling from his hands. Illegitimate child. The words echoed through his brain. He'd never heard those particular words but he'd heard the tone often enough. Indian child. Monster. Freak. He couldn't bear the thought of innocent little Joshua enduring the same ridicule and cruel mocking. There was one way to prevent it. He would offer them a home back at the farm where they would be safe from such taunts.

First he had to find Vivian. He edged forward, looking from one side to the other. No sign of her. Where could she have disappeared to in such a short time? She wouldn't have gone far carrying the baby and dragging the basket.

He reached the end of the block. Still no sign of her. The church lay ahead. The hospital farther away. To his right, more houses. To his left and down the street, the livery stable. *God, show me where she is. Help me find her.*

A flicker of movement caught his eye. He turned toward the little cemetery at the back corner of the churchyard. There she was, crouched down in the snow.

"Vivian." She couldn't hear him. But the cry wasn't for her. It came from the depths of his being. He drove to the church fence, jumped from the wagon and strode through the snow to her side. He knelt beside her, wrapped his arms about both her and Joshua.

She turned her face into his shoulder and wept.

He closed his eyes against her pain. He would do everything he could to protect her. For always.

She cried until she was spent. Still, she clutched his jacket front.

He patted her back and held her, letting her work out her sorrow.

She finally spoke, her voice muffled against his shoulder. "I've made such a mess of things."

Billy wanted to say she shouldn't blame herself. If anyone were to blame it was Wayne. Something was off about the Styleses though he'd readily allow he had his own reasons for disliking them. But to deny your own flesh and blood. *I got what I wanted a year ago.* He'd never before been tempted to use his size to hurt someone but Wayne made him want to make an exception.

"You didn't do this alone."

She sniffled. "But it appears I will have to deal with it alone."

He eased her back so he could look into her face. Seeing her tearstained cheeks and reddened eyelids hurt more than he could imagine. He'd hammered his thumb with less pain. He kissed each cheek, capturing the remnants of her tears with his lips.

Her eyes flooded with uncertainty as he lifted his head and looked deep into her eyes.

"You won't be alone. You have me."

"What do you mean?"

"I'm taking you back home. I'll take care of you and this little fellow."

"But your ma?"

He pulled his lips back in a mocking grin. "Ma's getting used to you." She'd likely have a conniption when Billy brought her back yet again. But she'd just have to accept this was the way it was going to be. He wanted to make the arrangement permanent but it was too early to talk to Vivian of such things.

A thread of pleasure wound itself around his pain at how she'd been treated. Perhaps it was possible to have his dream. This seemed a gift from God. Especially considering where they were. "What are you doing here?"

She turned, pointed toward the crude wooden crosses. "This is where my parents are buried."

He could make out their names carved into the wood.

"If I can ever afford it, I want to put up proper stone markers."

The cold seeped through his bones. "You're going to freeze sitting here. So am I. Come on, let's go home." He pulled her to her feet, kept her tucked against his side as he led her to the wagon. He lifted her to the seat, wrapped the blankets more tightly around Joshua, who slept peacefully. "Wouldn't want this little guy getting cold."

A sob tore from Vivian's throat. "He called my baby illegitimate."

Billy jumped up beside her and pulled her into his arms. "We'll protect him from that kind of talk."

She sniffed and sat up. "You know what else he said?"

Billy prayed Wayne hadn't been as harsh to Vivian as he'd been to him but he sensed the man would get an unholy delight out of hurting Vivian.

"He said our business was completed a year ago. As if he'd set out to take advantage of my neediness. Not that I'm excusing my behavior. I'll live the rest of my life regretting it. But wasn't it cruel to make it sound like I was just a...a..." Her voice broke along with the outer shell of Billy's heart. "As if I was just some dirty, despicable task he had to do."

Billy kept one arm around Vivian, shielding her from curious stares as they made their way out of town. He hoped anyone who saw him would be too interested in him to note the woman at his side. They took the back way from town and passed only two people, who seemed in a hurry to attend to their own business and barely glanced in Billy's direction.

He hadn't had time to think of it before but Wayne's statement did seem odd. As if he had set out to win Vivian's favor and once he had, considered he'd achieved his goal. He could think of no reason why Wayne should even care about Vivian. It just didn't make sense even for a worm like Wayne.

Chapter Eleven

Vivian leaned against Billy's chest, grateful for his support, both physical and emotional. When she'd learned Wayne was married, she'd fled in panic feeling like she had dropped off the world into nothingness.

And to hear from his mouth the very words she'd counted on him to protect Joshua from…

Panic swirled around her again and she pressed her face to Billy's jacket.

She had run, with no place to go. She didn't know how she ended up at her parents' graves. *Momma, Poppa. Why did you have to die and leave me homeless?*

Oh, if they knew the shame and sorrow she'd known since their deaths…

Being shunted off to the foundling home had been a shock she would never forget. She'd always been loved. Not so in the home. Children were simply stored there, made to earn their keep as much as possible, taught they were of no value to anyone and certainly not to society as a whole.

Working at the Weimers' had been a little different, except the work was harder.

And now—she groaned and Billy tightened his arm around her shoulders—she was powerless to stop her precious son from facing an even worse situation.

Only Billy cared. And perhaps understood like no other. She'd go home with him and accept his kindness. She couldn't think past that. They reached the lane. She sat up and faced the house. Her insides had calmed somewhat with Billy's comfort but she now began to shiver so hard she felt dizzy.

Billy might welcome her back.

But even though they had settled into an uneasy coexistence, she doubted Mrs. Black would feel the same as Billy about Vivian's return.

They stopped at the house. She turned to look up at Billy. When she saw he stared at the door with a troubled look on his face, her fears exploded. "Your ma."

"She'll be fine."

His tight words did nothing to reassure Vivian but he jumped down and went around to take Joshua from her arms, then lifted her to the ground.

She clung to his arm, dreading Mrs. Black's reaction.

Billy pushed the door back and they stood in the opening.

Mrs. Black saw Vivian and bolted to her feet. "You were supposed to leave her in town."

The anger in the woman's voice trickled acid through Vivian's insides. All she wanted was a place where she and Joshua were accepted and welcomed. Seems her sin made that impossible. She gritted her teeth to keep from crying out. She would live the rest of her life regretting her action. But it wasn't fair Joshua would also be punished when he had done nothing except be born out of wedlock. Something he could hardly be blamed for.

"Ma, things didn't work out. She has no place to go."

"You can't keep her. Already told you that."

Billy put Vivian's basket down. He shifted out of his coat while still holding Joshua, who had started to fuss.

Vivian thought to relieve him of her son but she couldn't make her muscles respond.

Billy hung his coat, then edged Vivian's cape from her shoulders and hung it.

"I said—"

"Ma, I'm keeping her. Come, Vivian." He edged her toward the big chair and eased her down.

She melted into the chair as weak as a piece of old yarn.

Ma stomped into her room and shut the door with a harsh click.

"You hold this fella while I get his bottle ready." He placed Joshua in her lap and folded her arms across him.

She blinked and focused her attention on her son. With a groan ripped from someplace so deep in her gut she couldn't begin to think where it originated, she caught Joshua to her chest and rocked.

She'd ruined his life.

Her sin was ever before her.

She didn't cry. She was all cried out. She didn't speak. There was nothing to say. She couldn't think. Couldn't face the weight of her failure.

Billy returned, knelt in front of her, caught her chin and waited for her to look at him. "You are safe here. For always."

She nodded. At least she had that—safety. And she had Billy's kindness. She pressed her hand to his as he held her chin. "I will never forget this."

He smiled. "Well, that's a start."

She wondered what he meant but didn't have a chance to ask as Joshua let her know he had waited long enough.

Billy handed her the bottle. "Feed the little man while I put away the horse and wagon." The door closed to signal he left.

Vivian sat alone with her little son—the evidence of her sin and the one who would bear the brunt of public censure. *Lord, I deserve it all. I know that. But Joshua? He's done nothing. Show me how to protect him.*

No one would make comments about Joshua out here on the Blacks' farm. He could grow up without hearing those unkind words. Was this God's answer?

Billy returned. He paced about the kitchen, opened the oven door and glanced inside. Grunted.

Ma called from her room but Vivian couldn't make out her words.

Slowly, it dawned on her. Billy hoped someone would cook supper. She reluctantly put Joshua in the little bed that still stood by the chair and wearily went to the stove. Food held no interest for her but the least she could do was meet Billy's needs.

Ma stomped from her bedroom to join them at the table. Her fierce frown made little impression on Vivian except to deepen her sense of failure.

Billy bowed his head. "Bless, O Lord, this food for Thy use, and make us ever mindful of the wants and needs of others. Amen."

A smile tugged at Vivian's mouth at his words and his ma's sound of disagreement. Some of her tension eased. She and Joshua were safe. Her son would be free of public disgrace here.

Sourness suddenly rolled in her stomach and she couldn't face the food she'd prepared. No matter where she went, where she lived, who she saw, Vivian knew she would never be free from the condemnation in her heart that had sentenced her son to a life of being shunned and ostracized. She pretended an appetite she didn't have to avoid attracting Billy's attention.

The next few days passed in a blur of emotions that tangled through her thoughts until she couldn't separate one from another—condemnation, determination, fear, hope and a sense of waiting.

Billy seemed to realize she needed time to heal, to recover and decide what was next.

Eventually, she began to think again. Not that she liked her thoughts. But she refused to look back. She had to plan a future for Joshua.

"Come to the barn with me," Billy said one morning, after he returned from doing chores.

She didn't need a second invitation. Joshua slept peacefully, allowing her to escape for a short time. The coat Billy had lent her still hung on the hook and she put it on.

He took her hand as they walked across the yard.

She liked how his hand engulfed hers. Suddenly, her heart stopped quivering with shock and returned to a normal beat. She liked this man. In fact, the only thing that had kept her from falling in love with him was she expected to marry Wayne. A plan that died a sudden death.

She no longer had to feel guilt at her fondness for Billy and she laughed with reborn hope.

He swung their connected arms. "I gotta tell you, that's the nicest sound I've heard in a long time."

"What?" She guessed he meant her laugh but wanted him to say so.

"I like to hear you happy." His voice deepened with what she took for tenderness. A peculiar sweetness washed through her heart, not quite erasing the shame and regret of her past, but cleansing it of some of its pain.

"I like to be happy."

They reached the barn but stood outside, the sun shining down on them with late-winter warmth. He pulled her around to face her. Her back pressed to the wood of the door. He rested his hands on either side of her without touching her and yet she felt as if he wrapped her in a protective embrace. He smiled down at her, his expression full of pleasure. "I'd like to make you happy every day of your life."

His words blessed her in a way that defied explanation. She couldn't speak. At least not with her mouth. She was certain her eyes spoke more than she knew or understood.

He leaned forward and brushed his lips to hers. A gentle, promising kiss. Warmth radiated from her mouth until it reached the far, secret places of her heart where her need for love and acceptance lay buried.

He lifted his head and searched her eyes. He must have read her surprise though she felt so much more.

"It's too soon to give an answer, but I'd like to marry you and give you and Joshua the protection of my name."

She nodded, still speechless.

He gave her another quick kiss, took her hand and led her into the barn. He talked about the cats. Told her the history of each one. Told her about dogs before and after Limpy. Twice he apologized for running over at the mouth, as he put it.

"I don't mind. It's interesting to hear your stories." Even more, she enjoyed being able to admire the gentle side of this big man. Like he said, it was too soon to make a commitment, but she liked the idea of his gentle strength being available for both her and Joshua.

The next few days, he seemed to delight in sharing every detail of his life with her. He took her for walks, carrying Joshua in his arms and explaining things to the baby as well as to Vivian.

Evenings—after he'd read the Bible out loud and his ma had gone to her room—continued to be the best part of the day as far as she was concerned.

One night, he pulled the Bible from the shelf again as she fed Joshua his bottle. "Vivian, I want to share something with you. Something I hope will ease the pain of your past." He turned the pages. "Psalm fifty-one." He started reading. She found the Psalms comforting and settled back to enjoy them.

He read, "'My sin is ever before me. Against thee, thee only, have I sinned, and done this evil—'"

She cried out as guilt swamped her. "Stop. Why are you reading this? I will never forget what I've done. I will never stop feeling guilty. I've not only sinned against God, I've brought shame and pain to my innocent child. I don't need a reminder. Why? Why would you do this?" Her insides churned with the pain of his unkindness. "I thought you understood. Accepted. What do you want from me?"

Billy bolted from the chair and knelt at her feet, squeezing her shoulders. "No. I am not accusing you. Never. I told you before, only one who is sinless has the right to judge and God, the righteous judge, does not condemn. That's why I wanted to read this to you. That's how King David felt after he'd sinned with Bathsheba. But he learned it wasn't the end of the story. Listen to the rest of the chapter." He pulled the Bible to her lap and ran his finger down the page until he found the place. "I'm going to skip some so you hear what David discovered. 'Create in me a clean heart; O God…Restore to me the joy of thy salvation; and uphold me with thy free spirit…Deliver me from blood-guiltiness, O God, thou God of my salvation.' See, it's a psalm of healing and forgiveness. God is saying He is willing to set you free from your guilt. He forgives you."

He ran his blunt fingertip across her cheek. "You can leave your past behind and start over."

Forgiveness, freedom. Could she even dream of such things? Not from what people said, she knew that, but from the accusation of her own heart? "Is it really possible?"

"It is. What's more, I think God is anxious to give it to you."

"It's a gift beyond comprehension."

"It is. But so is the gift of salvation. And if God did not spare His Son in order to provide us that gift, won't He even more readily forgive our sins as His children?"

"I never thought of it like that."

"Maybe you should."

She touched one of his wayward curls, let herself drink in every detail of this generous-hearted man. His broad, friendly face, the kindness in his eyes that blessed and loved her. She examined several more curls before she rested her hand on his shoulder. "Billy, you are the kindest man I've ever met."

He sobered. "It's not hard being kind to you 'cause I love you. I'm waiting for you to say you'll marry me."

She loved him, too. "I need to work through what you've just told me about God. I need to figure out who I am before I can be who you want me to be."

At that, he laughed. "I don't want you to be anything or anybody but who you are right now. But I'm willing to give you whatever time you need to work things out."

"Thank you. You're a good man."

He pulled her head down and kissed her slow and gentle. Billy would always be gentle. She knew that and she returned his kiss with a heart bursting with gratitude and hope—hope that she could be free from her guilt and free to start over.

Joshua screamed.

Vivian sighed. "Here we go again."

"Give him to me." Billy took him and began his nightly routine of walking and singing to the baby.

She watched him with her son. She loved him. She was certain of that. But could she make him happy? What had he said? That he liked her as she was. The idea gave her newfound delight. So much had happened in such a short time that she needed to sort it all out before she could give Billy the answer he wanted. And that she, too, wanted.

If Billy was at the house, he wanted to hold Vivian and tell her over and over how much he loved her. So, he would go to the barn where he'd tell Limpy. But after a few minutes in the barn, he would head back to the house to see Vivian and hold Joshua. And watch Ma shake her head in a pitying way.

Billy walked to the creek just so he could think. He'd be the first to admit he was acting like a man in love. And it felt good.

Every day he watched Vivian grow stronger, more confident. Every day he prayed for her to realize her sin did not stop God's love any more than it stopped Billy's. He'd gladly give her what she needed—home and belonging. And what her son needed—a name and a father.

Soon she'd be ready to forget the past and stride into the future, hand in hand with Billy.

He stood on the creek bank for a few minutes, paying scant attention to the pools of water on the ice. Spring would soon be here. A time of renewal and growth. He couldn't wait, though he didn't mean just nature with the soon-to-appear flowers and leaves, green grass and baby animals. He prayed it would be a time of renewal for Vivian, as well.

He knew she loved him and he anticipated the day she would agree to marry him.

Settled somewhat in his thoughts, he returned home in time for the noon meal. Vivian continued to prepare meals that satisfied in every way. And every meal he told her how much he appreciated her cooking.

Each time she would look pleased. "It's my pleasure. I like cooking."

"Good thing." He chuckled.

They had just finished when he heard a horse approaching and bolted to his feet. He'd never be comfortable with people visiting. "Someone coming," he called from the window.

Ma pushed her chair back and scurried to the middle of the room. "Why are so many people coming here?" She gave Vivian an accusing look.

Billy sighed before he turned back to the window. "Ma, you don't even know why he's come. Looks like the sheriff. Wonder what he wants."

"Go see," Ma said. "Tell him whatever he wants we don't have it. Tell him to leave us alone."

Billy was already on his way out the door. He strode

a few feet from the house and met the sheriff, waited as the man dismounted. "What can I do for you?"

Sheriff pushed his hat back. "I got a complaint about a young woman I hear is living here."

Vivian? She'd done nothing wrong. "First I heard the law cared who I let live in my house."

"If it's just Miss Halliday, the law don't care. But if she's got a baby boy with her…"

"Sheriff." His voice came out soft but full of unmistakable warning. "What is it you're trying to say?"

"I hear tell she stole the baby."

"Now who would tell you such a thing?"

"Does it matter?"

"Seems to me someone is trying to make trouble where there ain't any." He suspected Wayne was at the root of this interference.

"You gonna let me speak to the woman?"

He heard the warning in the man's voice. "Do I have a choice?"

"No."

"The baby is hers."

"If she can prove that, then no problem. But I have to be certain. Kidnapping is a mighty serious crime."

If Billy were a vengeful man he'd make Wayne pay for this. But he'd learned long ago the futility of trying to give an eye for an eye. "Come along."

He led the sheriff up the steps and into the house. Sheriff yanked off his hat. "G'day, Mrs. Black."

Ma's eyes grew wide, she scurried to the bedroom and slammed the door.

"See she's still some jittery."

Billy almost laughed. Jittery was like saying there's a bit of breeze across the Dakotas.

"And this is Miss Halliday, I presume."

She stood in the middle of the room, clutching the baby to her chest as if she expected the sheriff would snatch him away.

"Vivian, the sheriff wants proof Joshua is your son."

"I got proof." She edged toward the basket holding baby things and dug into the contents to pull forth a piece of paper, which she handed to the sheriff.

He read it slowly. "I see your name as the mother. No name for the father?"

Vivian's face drained of color. "No."

The sheriff cleared his throat. "This is proof enough. I'll not bother you anymore. Your papers are in order." He hesitated at the doorway, his hat suspended from his fingers. "Miss Halliday, you need not hide out here. No one will threaten you in town."

He turned once more. "I'll inform Mr. Styles that there is no reason for concern."

"Wayne sent you out?" Vivian whispered.

"No, the senior Mr. Styles. Good day."

They stared after him until they could no longer hear the sound of horse hooves.

Vivian turned into Billy's arms and he held her tight. "Everything is fine. No one will bother us again."

She nodded against his shoulder. "I can't believe Wayne told his father. And why would he care if I was out here?"

"I don't know. Maybe he thinks you'll make trouble for Wayne."

"I don't care if I ever see the man again. I only hope no one figures out he's Joshua's father. He's not the kind of man I want Joshua to look up to."

Billy vowed he'd do all in his power—with God's help—to be the sort of man Joshua *could* look up to.

Ma stumbled from the room looking as if she'd endured a vicious ordeal. She made it to the rocking chair and collapsed.

"Ma?"

She moaned. "Will it never end?"

"The sheriff won't be back."

"Don't mean the sheriff." She rocked so fast it made Billy dizzy.

"Ma?"

She shook her head and stared into the distance.

He shuddered. She hadn't been like this since the first day Vivian had entered their house. Why did such harmless things set her off?

Joshua fussed and Vivian laid him in the little bed as she prepared his bottle. Angry at being made to wait, Joshua screamed.

Ma sat in the rocker and as the baby's demands grew louder, she rocked harder. Pressing her hands to her ears, she made a mournful sound in the back of her throat.

Billy moved toward his mother as Vivian picked up the baby.

"Hush, now. You're not going to starve," Vivian murmured.

Joshua continued to raise his rather sturdy voice in protest as Vivian changed him.

Billy pulled his stool close to the rocker, watching Ma. Her distress never failed to make him feel power-less. Seems he could never do enough to help her. She lived with memories and hauntings that refused to leave her. As he watched, he prayed silently for her peace of heart.

Joshua stopped crying as Vivian stuck the bottle in his mouth, but Ma continued to rock and moan.

"Ma, what's wrong?"

She stopped rocking and listened. When she realized the baby had quit crying, she lowered her hands and stared straight ahead. As if looking into the past.

Billy shuddered.

"I had a baby." Her voice cracked on the words.

"I know, Ma. Fourteen pounds of baby." He grinned at Vivian. "I was the biggest baby they ever saw."

He laughed at the way Vivian's eyes grew round. Fourteen pounds was a lot of baby.

"Not you," Ma said, and began to rock. "I had another baby." She rocked harder. "When the Indians took me, I had a baby in my belly." She rocked so hard the chair creaked. "It was a little boy." She paused. "Much smaller than you as a baby." She resumed her frantic back-and-forth movement.

Billy struggled to accept this news. "A baby brother. What happened to him?"

Ma wailed and rocked harder and harder until Billy put his hand on the arm of the chair and stopped it.

"Ma, where's my brother?" If the Indians had him, Billy would get him back. Nothing would stop him.

Chapter Twelve

M a sat perfectly still, her face a flour-colored pallor. He wondered if she even breathed.

"Ma, tell me."

Her shoulders fell. Her face seemed to crumple like a log dying into ashes. "He's dead. The Indians took him from me. They—they killed him right in front of my eyes." She buried her face in her hands and moaned like a tortured animal.

Shock ran through Billy in one powerful wave that rattled him from head to toe. Pictures flooded his mind of a baby—his brother—being killed. He closed his eyes. He didn't want to think about it. For sure he didn't want to see it inside his head. *Oh, God, stop this awful thing.* He meant the memories, the pain, the imaginations.

Ma's eyes were glassy. Billy shook her. "Ma, it's okay. It wasn't your fault."

She moaned, a sound so mournful Billy's heart squeezed like a giant fist. He rubbed her back.

"That's why I can't bear the baby's crying."

Before Billy could guess her intent, Vivian placed Joshua in Ma's lap, holding Ma's arms around the baby.

Ma shivered. She pulled back until she stared at Vivian who nodded, her eyes intent.

Ma lowered her gaze to the baby. At that moment, Joshua smacked his lips, smiled and cooed. With a moan that sounded half prayer, Ma cradled the baby to her chest. A look of surprise and wonder filled her face. She touched Joshua's cheek cautiously then smiled and relaxed, holding the baby as if doing so filled her heart.

Vivian handed her the bottle. "He isn't finished eating."

Ma fed Joshua, her eyes never leaving the baby's face. The baby studied her intently as he sucked. He smiled around the nipple, letting milk run down his chin.

Ma laughed. "He's a little scamp." Her voice broke and her eyes began to leak.

Billy scrubbed the back of his hand over his cheeks, surprised to feel them damp. He seemed to be leaking, too, and he ducked his head to hide his embarrassment. But when he stole a glance at Vivian, she wasn't looking at him. She smiled at his ma, and if he didn't miss his guess, her eyes were awash, too.

He settled back on the stool and watched Ma feeding Joshua. She alternately smiled at the baby and then sobered, her lips quivering.

Billy silently prayed for God to use this to heal Ma's hurts. Though he didn't expect she could ever forget seeing her own baby murdered.

Joshua finished his bottle and Ma raised him to her shoulder to burp him. As she patted the tiny back, she shifted to look into Billy's face.

"I never even tried to stop them."

He guessed she meant the Indians when they took the baby from her. Her mouth worked and he understood she had more to say.

"I was—" She swallowed loudly. "I was—" Her voice fell to an agonized whisper. "I was glad he died. I didn't want him raised there." Her eyes were bottomless pools of self-loathing misery.

Billy wrapped his arms around Ma and Joshua. "You couldn't have done anything. It wasn't in your hands. The baby is with God now."

She laid her head against his shoulder. "I know."

Billy patted Ma's back a few times then released her.

"Read from the Bible," she said.

He pulled it from the shelf. He could think of no appropriate scripture for this situation and paused to ask God to direct him to something of comfort. He opened the Bible to the Psalms and began to read chapter sixty-eight. "'Let God arise, let his enemies be scattered; let them also that hate him flee before him.'" He read on, letting the words of comfort and assurance cleanse his soul from the shock and anger of learning he had a baby brother who had been brutally killed. He prayed Ma would receive the same comfort and assurance.

He read for a long time, psalm after psalm. "'Save me, O God; for the waters are come into my soul.'" It seemed he couldn't get enough of God's word, and the way Ma and Vivian sat quiet and contemplative led him to think they hungered for it as much as he.

It wasn't until Joshua stirred that Billy closed the Bible and returned it to the shelf.

"I'll take him," Vivian said.

Ma released the baby. "I'm very tired. I think I'll go rest."

Billy pushed to his feet and hugged her. "Ma, I love you."

"I love you, too, son." She patted his cheek then went to her room.

Billy scrubbed his hand over his hair. He felt as drained as if he'd run four days without food. In fact, he was starved. "I'm going to have some bread and jam. You want any?"

"No, thanks."

"Tea?"

"That would be fine." She concentrated on adjusting Joshua's nightie and putting his booties on again.

Billy busied himself at the stove. He seemed alternately fatigued and then bursting with energy that he knew not how to handle. For a moment, he considered going outside and chopping wood. Or at least making a trip to the barn. But inside him there was a wad of words that needed saying, for his sake not anyone else's.

He carried tea to Vivian, who sat in the rocker holding Joshua, then he settled in the stuffed chair and attacked the stack of bread he'd slathered with jam. "Ma made this jam."

"It's good."

"Ma works hard."

"It shows. The sausages, the butter, the quilt."

He took a gulp of hot tea. "She's never said much about when she was with…them. I always figured she didn't want to remember."

"Can you ever forget the past?"

He didn't have a satisfactory answer and it left him floundering. "I don't know. I simply don't know." He wanted to forget the past. Wasn't sure he wanted to think too far into the future, either. "Seems we should do our best to enjoy each new day. God's word says, 'This is the day which the Lord hath made; we will rejoice and be glad in it.'"

She smiled. "That sounds like something Marie would say." She grew thoughtful, her gaze on Joshua. "The past is always with us. Look at your ma. It's been with her for so many years."

The way pain shafted through him felt like he'd stepped on a foot-long nail. He wanted to help Ma. He wanted to help Vivian. He didn't know how except to love them and pray for them.

Something about the sheriff's visit hovered at the back of his mind, a distant troubling voice. "What was it Wayne said to you when you saw him?"

Her eyes grew wide with shock. "That awful word about Joshua?"

"No. The other."

She considered the question. "About our business being completed a year ago? I assume he meant…" Her face deepened to the color of a summer rose.

He examined all the things that had been said. "Didn't Wayne's father say something similar when you saw him in the bank?"

"Yes." Her brow furrowed. "Isn't that strange?"

Billy wondered if it were more than that. "You said you signed some papers for Wayne?"

"Yes."

"Did you read them carefully?"

Again that flush of pink. "No. I trusted Wayne when he said they were only to erase the debt my parents left."

"I wonder…"

"What?"

"I wonder if there wasn't something more to those papers you signed."

"Like what?"

"I have no idea." The whole afternoon had been so

full of shock after shock he could no longer think clearly. "I'll give it some thought."

Vivian couldn't imagine why Wayne or anyone would want her to sign papers that were other than what he said. And if they were other, why would he go to such lengths? Surely, Billy was being suspicious on account of his dislike for the Styleses—a dislike Vivian was learning to share.

She dismissed the whole affair as being nothing more than mistaken reaction. Right now, she had bigger things to consider.

Was it possible God would forgive her sin? Yes, she believed it but…

But did she? Her thoughts went round and round in ceaseless questions. She stared out the window. If she could be alone to think and pray.

Billy returned from doing his chores.

She barely waited for him to step into the house. "Would you mind watching Joshua while I go for a walk? I need to think."

He grinned and touched her chin. "Gladly. Nothing like a walk to ease a person's mind. Take your time. Little Josh and I can amuse each other."

She pulled on the warm coat and boots then headed out following the path to the creek. She reached her destination, found a grassy spot, pulled the back of her coat under her and sat. The air was so clear she could hear birds rattling about in the branches overhead.

Puddles of mirrorlike water lay in spots on the blue ice. She breathed deeply, cleansing her lungs. *Lord, I need to talk to You. I need to understand what is happening to me. What You want. Where You want me. I need Your help to consider the future.*

She'd messed things up badly enough trying to do things her way. And now she had a baby son to think about. She couldn't afford to make another mistake that would affect him the rest of his life.

Peace and quietness surrounded her and she slowly exposed her worries to God.

My past. Can You truly forgive my past?

Forgive us our trespasses as we forgive those who trespass against us.

She had to forgive Wayne. She'd never blamed him for his part in her sin knowing she had the choice to say yes or no, but he had taken advantage of her hunger for love. Even that didn't make her angry. What she found impossible to forgive was that he would deny his son, call him that awful name.

They called God's son the same awful name.

"Oh, God, I guess I can't refuse to forgive when You do. I can't expect You to forgive me if I can't forgive others. Here before You, I forgive Wayne. I know I won't find it easy to forget what he's done. In fact, I never will. Not when every time I look at Joshua I have a reminder."

She also knew she would have to constantly remind herself of the decision she had made this day.

"Now am I forgiven?"

A verse that Billy had read some days ago whispered across her thoughts. *Neither do I condemn thee.*

She shook her head. God might forgive and let her into heaven but there was no forgiveness on earth for what she'd done.

She just had to move forward. Which necessitated her deciding what to do about her future. She loved Billy, knew she and Joshua would be safe with him, but something played at the back of her mind. Something she couldn't quite capture and name. And until she did…

She returned to the house two hours later, her mind made up, her spirit strengthened by the time she'd spent in prayer. Tonight, she would tell Billy her decision.

She waited until Joshua slept on Billy's chest and Billy leaned back, patting the baby's tiny backside. Such a good, gentle man. He had so much to give— so much love and tenderness. Her throat tightened till she could hardly breathe. He deserved nothing but happiness. Was he really content hiding out here?

All afternoon she had thought of how to say the words to him. She had prayed, was certain of what she had to do, but suddenly none of her rehearsed speeches felt right. She loved him. It ought to be all that mattered.

He shifted his bulk.

It pained her that he thought others considered him

a monster solely because of his size. If only they knew. If only he would give them a chance to discover it.

Time was running out for her to speak. And she didn't want to put it off to scratch at the back of her mind another day. "Billy, I did some serious thinking today."

His hand grew still. He watched her with a mixture of eagerness and caution.

Oh, how she dreaded hurting him. But perhaps he would listen to her plan. Agree to some changes. "Something the sheriff said has been bothering me. He said I didn't need to hide."

Billy opened his mouth.

"Let me finish. Part of me feels like I must. But I can't. I can't." She closed her heart to the way Billy's jaw muscles bunched up. "Hear me out." She drew in a slow breath and tried to sort out her feelings, rearrange her thoughts, find the right words instead of this sensation that everything inside had turned into hail stones bouncing about aimlessly, striking everyplace at once without warning, without reason. "I want to say this so you understand, so be patient while I try and sort out everything."

He didn't move. Didn't give any indication of what he felt.

She knew he had pulled shutters over his thoughts, allowing nothing to show in his eyes or expression. "I know what I did was shameful and marks Joshua. I expect all his life he will hear that horrible word. But

I am not ashamed of him. He's a precious child. I pray he grows into a strong young man able to face challenges and ignore hurtful things so he can focus on what's important." She had to break through Billy's icy reserve and knelt in front of him, pressing her hands to his knees. "Billy, I love you but if I hide here, I will be saying to Joshua that I am ashamed of him. I will teach him to be ashamed of who he is."

Billy's expression grew more distant as he pulled farther and farther away from her.

She leaned forward, cupped her hands to the sides of his face. "Billy, I love you. You are the kindest, most gentle man I will ever meet."

He shook his head in disagreement but the movement also shook her hands away.

She settled back on her heels.

"I guess that means no to my offer of marriage." His words were little bullets of pain.

"I don't want it to."

"Then what do you want?"

She knew what she wanted. With all her heart. "Billy, don't you think it's time you moved on?"

"Leave the farm?" His voice was low, giving away nothing of what he felt.

"No. I don't mean that. I mean, leave the past."

He snorted. "Can't leave the past when it won't leave us."

"Things change. People change."

"Haven't seen it."

"You say you're here to protect your ma but hiding from her past has only caused her pain. She's needed to confront it. Now she will start to heal."

"Ain't likely she'll forget about seeing her baby killed, now is it?"

"I don't mean she'll forget, but seems to me trying to hide it and pretend it didn't happen caused her unnecessary pain."

"You think if we parade through town we can pretend we don't hear what people say?"

"No. Yes. I don't know. I'm not saying what I mean."

"Then say it."

No mistaking the edge of anger to his words. She started over. "Billy, I love you but I can't hide Joshua out here. I want a normal life. I want to go to town proudly at your side. I want Joshua to be part of normal life. I want that for me. For you."

"I ain't going to make Ma go through torment just to try and be normal."

"Maybe it's time for a change. Maybe your ma is ready for it. You could give people a chance, you know."

"I gave them a chance. All they saw was an Indian woman and her monster son. Just 'cause I'm big don't make me a monster. 'Sides, Ma would never go to town."

"She might think differently if you ask her."

"I ain't asking her."

"Not even for me or our love?"

He shifted, pulled her close until she again rested her arms on his knees, looking up to him. "You could be happy here."

"Yes, I could. I could be happy anywhere with you."

He nodded. His eyes grew bright and he leaned forward to kiss her.

She closed her eyes as her love spread sweet honey throughout her heart.

"I love you," he whispered. "Can't it be enough?"

She wanted nothing more. For herself. But so much more for Joshua and so she let it go, praying Billy would think on what she'd said.

But two days later, nothing changed. Billy seemed set on proving his love. Not that he needed to and his tenderness left her feeling like a windblown tumble-weed, shifting to one thing when Billy was around—couldn't his love be enough?—to something else when he wasn't there—didn't Joshua need more? A chance to be accepted by those who would and the opportunity to learn there were those who wouldn't accept him but he could live with it. If they stayed here, she feared he would think there was only one opinion. She could not let him grow up believing everyone considered his birth a shame. Hiding out here would do exactly that.

She needed to talk to someone who could help her sort things out. "Who pastors the church now?"

"Pastor Morrow."

"Why, he was here when I was a child."

Billy laughed. "Still here."

"How is he?"

"Never heard anything indicating he was anything but fine."

She could remember the pastor in their house. He often came for dinner. How awed she'd felt when he said the table grace. Somehow, in her childish mind, she thought he spoke directly to God. She remembered other things, too. How he'd asked about her relationship with God and encouraged her to read the Bible and always speak to God. He had stood at the front of the church and held out his hand to her as she went forward to tell the congregation she had put her faith in Jesus as her savior. She was only eleven years old. Mother had said she didn't have to go to the front for her faith to be real, but she'd wanted to and Pastor Morrow had agreed she could. How she'd shaken as she faced the people in the pews—so many people with gray hair. It seemed they were all frowning. And her school friends grinned in either curiosity or teasing. The pastor had squeezed her hand. Her courage had returned and she'd said her piece. Couldn't remember a word of it now. But she remembered how speaking publicly had made her faith seem more real than ever.

She suddenly ached to see this old family friend.

"Would it be possible for me to borrow the wagon and go to town?" Vivian asked the next day.

Her request reverberated through Billy like a clap

of thunder. It had been several days since she had said she wanted a normal life, but she'd said nothing more and he sort of hoped she'd changed her mind about it. He'd sure gone out of his way to prove they could have a rich and full life right here. What did they need with other people? Why would she want Josh to put up with the unkind words he'd hear? And he'd hear them. Better to protect the little guy. Give him lots of love. Lots of things to do. Just like he'd been showing Vivian. She seemed to enjoy walking with him, helping him with his pets. He'd even started training the young colt simply for the joy of showing Vivian how to work with the animal.

"I could walk if you aren't keen to let me drive the wagon." Vivian's words jolted him into considering an answer.

"You ever drive a wagon before?" He 'spected she had but he was stalling for time.

"A time or two when the Weimers needed someone to take a wagon to the mill or bring something back. I can handle it, I assure you."

He nodded. Knew she expected more than that. But for the life of him, he couldn't think of letting her go to town. Could she be setting out to find a different place to live?

"I want to see Pastor Morrow. I need to talk to him."

Pastor Morrow? His chest half caved in with relief. "I'll take you."

"No need."

"Got to pick up some things." They stood in the kitchen doing the dishes together and he glanced out the window. The warm weather of a few days ago had ended. It was sunny but cold. "I don't much care for the idea of taking Joshua all that way and back again. It's too hard on him."

He turned to study Ma as she poured milk into the cat dishes. Purring and the crackle of the fire were the only sounds. Comforting as they normally were—caught between worry about what Vivian said about not wanting to stay on the farm and concern for Joshua—this morning they jangled across his nerves.

Ma looked up from washing the milk things. "You leave that little feller here where he'll be warm and safe. I'll look after him."

Vivian jerked her gaze to Billy. They stared at each other and silently considered the offer. Ma seemed as sane as anyone since her confession about seeing her baby murdered. She'd fed Joshua several times and always held the baby tenderly. Billy figured she had conquered one of her demons. He sensed she'd protect the baby with her life if need be to make up for not being able to save her own infant.

But was it too soon to expect Ma to cope with this much change?

"Stop worrying about me," Ma said.

Although not completely at ease about leaving Joshua, they'd been fortunate the baby hadn't suffered from exposure in his adventures. Vivian gave a slight nod.

"Okay, Ma. You can look after the baby while we go to town."

The two of them bundled up and hurried to the barn where Billy hitched up Blaze.

Vivian paced from the wagon to the door, clutching her hands before her. "I'm not being foolish, am I?"

Billy sighed. "It's impossible to believe you can have a normal life in town. No one will let you. I can testify to that."

She spun around, stared at him like he rattled away in a foreign language, then burst out laughing.

"What's so funny?" He was being completely serious. Speaking from the hunger of his heart. It kind of stung that she found it amusing.

"I was thinking about whether it was safe to leave Joshua with your mother. After all, it's only been a few days since she wouldn't so much as look at him."

He ducked away to hide his embarrassment at being caught thinking of how to persuade her to stay while she was thinking of something else entirely. "Ma would protect him with her life to make up for losing her own baby." The knowledge he'd had a younger brother he never even got to meet knuckled through his insides.

Vivian nodded and stared at the side of the wagon. "I guess so. Unless something upsets her. Then what?"

"She ain't crazy."

"Oh, Billy. I know that. But you got to admit she's pretty spooked around strangers. After all, she seldom sees one."

"Seen her share the last little while."

"And she's managed fine. Maybe…"

He heard the hesitation in her voice and prepared himself for more arguments.

"Maybe it's time for a change. Time to persuade her to widen her world. Perhaps just a step at a time."

He led Blaze out and helped Vivian to the wagon seat. "You think she can be normal? That anyone will ever think I'm normal? And don't be fooling yourself. No one will ever let you forget you have a son without the benefit of a husband."

His words hurt her. He could tell by the way she sat up straight, looking neither to the right nor the left and tried to shrink into herself so her shoulder didn't rub his. The last thing he wanted was to give her pain. "Let's not argue and ruin the day."

She kind of collapsed forward and let her breath out in an airy sigh. "You're right." She turned suddenly and faced him, her face gleaming with determination. "I believe our love will find a way."

He took her hand. He wanted to believe as stubbornly as she but he couldn't forget she'd said she wanted a normal life. So long as she insisted on that, how could their love be? His teeth felt bathed in vinegar. He'd been alone so long. Ached for more for years. And here it was within reach. Except for who he and Ma were—the Indian woman and her monster son.

He hated the taunts. Hated how it made him feel powerless despite his size, which didn't defend him against unkind words. Even so, he might have put up with what they said about him. But not how they tormented Ma. She hadn't shown her face in town in five years or more. He quit even asking because it upset her so much.

Chapter Thirteen

Vivian knocked on the door of the manse as Billy waited in the wagon to be sure someone was home.

Mrs. Morrow opened the door. "Yes?"

Vivian recognized the woman immediately. "Do you remember me? Vivian Halliday?"

"Vivian!" The woman pulled her to her ample bosom and hugged her tight. "I wondered if we'd ever see you again. You know, I think of you often and have prayed God would uphold you. Child, how have you been?"

Vivian clung to the woman, the scent of peppermint triggering a burst of memories. Mrs. Morrow had taught Sunday school and handed out peppermint candies to good little boys and girls. Vivian had always earned one. This poor saint of a woman would be shocked to discover that Vivian was no longer a good girl.

She remembered Billy waited and turned to wave him away. He planned to visit his friend Lucas while Vivian visited at the manse.

"Come in, child. Come in." Mrs. Morrow led her into the well-used parlor.

Again, Vivian was assaulted by memories. "The horsehair sofa." She remembered the feel of the hide against her legs, rough, poking through her clothing if she didn't sit just right on it. And slippery if she sat so the hair all ran smoothly toward the floor. When Mother wasn't looking, she liked to slide downward.

Mrs. Morrow chuckled. "You were like every other child who liked to slip and slide on it."

Vivian giggled. "I didn't think you noticed."

The woman gave a sideways hug. "I didn't mind in the least. Now sit down. I'll make tea and you can tell me what you've been doing."

Vivian chose the little chair with wooden arms and pink-and-rose brocade upholstery on the seat and back. She looked about at the room, seeing a few new things like the picture of the Morrows' grandchildren and a painting of a prairie sunset.

The woman returned with a large silver tea tray.

"Is the pastor around?"

"He's upstairs studying but I've called him. He'll join us in a minute. He's as anxious to hear what you have to say as I am."

Vivian pretended a great interest in adjusting her skirts so they lay neat. They might be less pleased to see her once they heard her story. She lifted her head, her breath stalling in her throat as she heard footsteps descending the stairs. And then the pastor entered the room. His gaze fell on Vivian and a welcoming smile creased his face.

"Vivian, my dear child."

She rose and went into his arms, struggling to control her emotions. This dear elderly couple was so much a part of her childhood that she felt like she had almost returned home. A lump landed heavily in the bottom of her stomach at the shame she must confess.

Mrs. Morrow poured tea and handed Vivian a dessert plate with a generous slice of lemon cake.

Vivian laughed. "This was always my favorite. I remember worrying when we had church socials that I wouldn't get a piece before it was all gone."

"The good Lord knew you were coming today."

Vivian hadn't realized she'd sighed so loudly until the pastor patted her hand.

"I'm glad you're back. Whatever is burdening you, we're here to help, but first, enjoy your cake."

Vivian welcomed the chance to sort her thoughts. This time, she could voice them to two gentle friends. She finished her cake and put aside the plate. "I guess you know I went to a foundling home."

Mrs. Morrow grabbed her hand. "We both had the flu at the time or we wouldn't have let it happen. For a while, I wasn't sure Mr. Morrow was going to survive." Her voice thickened.

"I'm glad he did." Otherwise, she would have no one to turn to now.

Slowly, one strangled word after another, she told her sordid story. "I'm so ashamed of what I did but I don't want Joshua to think I'm ashamed of him. I fear if I stay on the farm with Billy and his ma that is exactly what I am teaching him." For a moment, she couldn't go on, as her throat closed off with sorrow and regret. Her poor little son should not be made to pay for something his mother had done. "I don't mind facing what people say. I deserve it. But how can I face what they say about my son? He's a beautiful little boy."

"Does his father know about him? That would seem the first avenue to pursue."

"He's not interested."

"I could speak to him. Remind him of his duty. Do we know the man?"

Vivian considered her answer carefully. "I don't ever want anyone to know who his father is."

"I understand. Your secret will be safe with us if you choose to reveal his identity."

She knew that. And she wanted to tell them. They might as well know the whole truth. "It's Wayne Styles."

To their credit, neither of them revealed shock or surprise, though they likely felt both.

"He's now married," she added unnecessarily. "So,

he can't do his duty to me and Joshua. And he doesn't want to. He made it very plain."

"So, you must face this on your own. Only you won't be on your own. You'll have our support and even more importantly, God's help."

"I don't expect God's help. I know I deserve whatever punishment He chooses to send my way. I only want to do what I can to protect Joshua, apart from hiding him."

Pastor Morrow slipped his chair closer. "Vivian, I can't say what people will say or think or how they will act but I can tell you what God says." He opened his Bible. "None of us is without sin."

Vivian nodded. Billy had said the same. But knowing she was like everyone else did not ease her sense of shame.

"Here in First John chapter one, verse nine, God's word says, 'If we confess our sins, he is faithful and just to forgive us our sins, and to cleanse us from all unrighteousness.' He will cleanse away the guilt of your sins. All of them."

"I hear the words. I know they are true. But…I don't know if they apply to me. I mean, this isn't like telling a lie or sassing your mother. This is a big sin."

"And one you can't hide or relegate to the past because of your son. Is that what you mean?"

"It is also one other people won't let me forget."

"The first thing to deal with is to believe that God forgives you. Do you believe that?"

She knew the correct answer was yes but did she believe it?

"God is in the forgiveness business."

Billy had said something similar when he'd pointed out that forgiving sins after they were God's children was no harder for God than forgiving for salvation.

"You must choose to believe God or not."

Was it really that simple? Just choosing. *Lord, God, is it really possible that You can forgive me for such an awful sin?* Would He have said it if He didn't mean it? All that stood in her way of forgiveness and cleansing was her lack of belief? "I don't know how to make myself believe it."

Mrs. Morrow leaned forward. "May I say something?"

Vivian nodded.

"I remember the day you chose to believe God for your salvation. You were always such a single-minded child. I had just finished a lesson explaining God's plan of redemption. You waited until the others left then said, 'I'm going to do it. I'm going to do what you said.' I thought I might have to walk you through a prayer or something but when I offered, you politely refused. 'It's done. I already decided.'"

"I remember."

"My mother used to say something. 'God said it. I believe it. That settles it.'"

Vivian replayed the words in her head and slowly she nodded. "I believe it." A swell of peace raced up her insides, caught in her throat, pushed at her tears. She blinked and laughed as a burst of joy exploded inside her.

Both of the dear folk reached for a hand. Pastor Morrow prayed aloud. "Heavenly Father, Merciful God, wonderful Savior, how we rejoice that Vivian has found the forgiveness You generously extend to each of us every day. Keep her joy strong and help her face the challenges of her life. Amen."

Vivian sobered. "I can face whatever life hands me but I don't know what the right thing is for Joshua."

"God will guide you."

Confront your accusers. The words were so clear Vivian knew immediately what she wanted to do and she told the Morrows.

"It's not necessary," the pastor said.

"I want to do it this way."

The Morrows looked at each other and smiled.

Mrs. Morrow spoke. "I'm not surprised. You've always been very clear about how you wanted to handle things, even as a child."

"You can certainly do it if you want."

She nodded. Now if God would just send a solution so Billy would consider living a normal life. She closed her heart to the pain her decision would bring if he continued to hide out at his farm.

The conversation shifted back to ordinary things— news of people she vaguely remembered, plans for an upcoming social, and as always on the prairie, talk about the weather.

Pastor Morrow refilled his tea cup. "I was surprised to hear you'd sold your house to the bank."

"Is that what I did?" She gave an embarrassed laugh. "Wayne brought out some papers for me to sign to get rid of my parents' debt at the bank."

The pastor's brow furrowed deeply. "How odd. If they had an outstanding debt against the property, the courts would have allowed them to sell the house years ago. They had an auction sale and sold the contents shortly after your parents died. Why would they wait to sell the house?"

Vivian knew nothing about legal proceedings but she wished she'd at least read those papers before she signed them. "All our things were sold?" She wondered what had happened to the family Bible and the pictures of Pinky and Blue Boy.

"Much of it went to friends and neighbors."

"I have nothing left of my family but I learned to live with that as an orphan." She was more fortunate than many of the children. At least she had experienced a loving mother and father. Some of them never had and never would. It had been that knowledge that spurred her to action on her son's behalf. She wouldn't let him grow up in the home thinking no one loved him.

Nor would she let him grow up thinking he was too shameful a secret to be out in public. Not even if she had to sacrifice her love for Billy. The thought dragged sharp stones through her heart and tossed them, blood-stained, to the bottom of her stomach where they exerted cruel pressure.

Billy headed the wagon out of town. His insides felt wound too tight all morning but seeing the smile on Vivian's lips and the determination in her eyes released some of the tension. Whatever she had discussed with the pastor had eased the strain that had been in her eyes for days.

"I take it you had a good visit."

"Very satisfactory." She explained how she'd decided to let God forgive her. "It's that simple. And that hard." She opened the tea towel containing the sandwiches she'd brought along and handed him a thick one filled with hefty slices of meat.

"How was your visit with Lucas?"

"Got a bunch more papers to read."

"That's nice." They continued in peaceful contentment.

"There's something about this business with Wayne and his father that isn't sitting right with me, so I asked Lucas about your parents' house. He said he found it mighty peculiar that the bank waited this long to sell it."

Vivian stopped eating. "Pastor Morrow said much the same." She told him what the good man had said.

Billy pulled back on the reins. He reached for

another sandwich. "This is getting more and more suspicious sounding. I think you should talk to a lawyer."

"A lawyer? What for?"

"Whatever you signed for, Wayne allowed them to sell the house. I think it's time to ask some questions."

She turned away. Stared into the distance. "I don't want to."

"Why not?"

She swallowed hard enough to make her throat bob. "Because it will prove how foolish I am to sign something without reading it." Slowly, she faced him, her eyes wide, her lips trembling. "Just because he was kind to me."

Her distress cracked him open from stem to stern. He folded her against his chest and rocked her. "Vivian, you were alone and lonely. It sounds to me like Wayne took advantage of that. But you don't have to be alone anymore. I'm here."

She nodded against his lapel, her fingers clutching the fabric of his coat.

He would protect her against all threats.

"Will you go with me to the lawyer?" She sat up, her gaze demanding so much from him.

Could he give her all she wanted? He didn't know but he would do his best.

He bent and kissed her, feeling the dampness on her cheeks from recent tears, tasting the salt on his lips. He wanted to head the wagon for home where he could protect her from the cruelness of life but she had asked this one thing of him. "I'll take you."

There was no back entrance to Mr. Legal's office so Billy gritted his teeth and headed down the street. He hadn't been this way for years. Suddenly, he realized he had been out in public view at least two times in the past few weeks—the first time to rescue Vivian from her stunned state in front of the bank, and the second when he'd heard Wayne was married and drove as fast as he could to the Styles house, not caring that people saw him. Was that close enough to normal for her?

He pulled the wagon to a halt and helped her down. She tucked her hand into the crook of his elbow.

He smiled. Knew if anyone saw him they would see a big goofy man with a tiny little gal at his side and shake their head in wonder, but he liked feeling big and protective with Vivian.

Inside the office, a man with glasses parked on his nose glanced up. "May I be of service?" He looked at Billy as he spoke.

Billy's smile fled. Vivian could speak for herself. "Miss Vivian Halliday would like your advice." Suddenly, he realized that neither of them had come prepared to pay the man cash. "If she can't pay you, I will."

"Fine. Now that we've taken care of the important things, why don't you both take a seat and tell me your problem."

Billy knew from the gleam in the man's eyes that

he was teasing about the money. It made Billy relax and he held a chair for Vivian then perched in the not-quite-adequate one at her side.

"It's about my parents' house," Vivian said, and told the lawyer the whole business.

Mr. Legal nodded, asked a few questions and made some notes.

Vivian finished and sat twisting her mittens into a knot. "I know I should have read the papers but I didn't. However, I did sign them so that would make them legal."

The man tapped the top of a square glass paper-weight. "I'll do some investigation and let you know. Where might I find you when I have news?"

"She's at our house." Billy made sure the lawyer heard *our*. "With Ma and me." He wanted to give no cause for gossip.

"I know where it is. When I have something I'll ride out and let you know."

"Thank you," Vivian whispered, and pushed to her feet. She waited until she sat on the hard seat of the wagon and they again rode away from town to speak again. "I don't know why I went there. I'm sure there is nothing to be done."

"Wouldn't it be nice to know the nature of those papers you signed?"

"It would ease my mind a bit."

"Well then, that's something." He draped his arm

across her shoulders and pulled her close, satisfied when she leaned against his chest.

"I had a good talk with the pastor."

"Good. It's nice to hear you more at ease."

"Letting God forgive me is a load off my mind."

He tightened his arm about her and kissed her head, wishing he could feel her silky hair instead of the woolen cape. His love for her filled him until he wondered how he would contain it.

"It was good to talk to someone who remembered my parents and recalled me as a little girl." She laughed gently. "They saw me as strong minded."

He chuckled. "Guess they knew you pretty well."

She gave his chest a playful slap. She sat up so suddenly he feared she would tumble from the wagon and grabbed her. "Billy, I want to go to church again. I'm…" She drew in a breath and seemed to hold it.

He sensed her fear and tried to pull her close.

She pressed her palms to his chest. "I've decided I am going to face the congregation and confess my sin."

"What? Why would you do that?"

"Because of something you said."

"Me?" He'd never stand in front of the mocking crowd. Knew the futility of it. People thought what they wanted, said what they wanted.

"Remember when you said Jesus said, 'neither do I condemn thee'?"

He'd told her that all right. Even read it from the

Bible. "It's got nothing to do with standing in front of the whole church."

Her smile was full of sweetness. "I figure if God doesn't condemn me then I have nothing to dread from people. Now, do I?"

"You'd think that's the way it should be. But it ain't."

She trailed a cool finger down his cheek. He should tell her to put her mittens on but not until she finished touching him—a touch that went far deeper than the pores of his skin. It landed somewhere south of his most distant thoughts and burrowed beneath all his secrets and longings, giving them life.

"Billy, I know you've endured so much but you are a good man. A man I'd be proud to walk into any business in town with. I want to let people see me with you. See what a good man you are. I want you to stop hiding at the farm."

"You want a normal life."

"Normal can be many things. But yes, I want to live proud of who I am, who my son is and proud of the man I love. Billy, you have no reason to hide."

He'd longed for such acceptance all his life. She offered it to him. But it came at a price. She wanted him to live in the open. "Your love makes me proud. But what you want is not possible. Don't you think I tried? I'm afraid this is as good as it gets." He had found what he wanted. Love. A chance to marry and have a family. But what she wanted wasn't possible.

They would soon be home. Somehow, in the next few minutes, he had to make her understand the truth.

"I can never abandon Ma. Never."

Vivian sat up. "Maybe she's ready to move on. I'll pray she's willing to change."

Easy for her to say. She'd never seen how Ma reacted to any suggestion of doing anything normal like going to town. "I hid in a cupboard when I was six and couldn't help her. I ain't gonna ever again do something to hurt her. I will stand by her as long as she lives."

He let the wagon slow to a snail's pace and turned to Vivian. "My normal is what you see. If you love me, you have to accept that." He waited, hoping against fear she would nod agreement. Instead, her eyes grew watery. Her lips trembled but her jaw muscles tightened. He knew before she spoke she would not give the answer he ached for. "I love you. I accept you but I can't hide. I have to give Joshua more than that."

Chapter Fourteen

Vivian knew there was no easy answer to their dilemma. She prayed Mrs. Black would change and Billy would believe it, even as he must believe her love despite her decision.

She watched Mrs. Black, hopefully assessing her behavior. They had arrived from their trip to town to find her contentedly rocking the sleeping baby. The older woman smiled as they stepped inside. "We had a good day."

The first, Vivian hoped, of many such days that took Billy's ma further from the comfortable cocoon she had buried herself in, and closer to starting a normal life.

She sensed Billy's restlessness in the way he shuffled the newspapers without reading them, and in the way he often hurried to the barn to see his pets. It hurt her clean through to think she caused him mental anguish.

"I want to see to the animals," he said yet again late one morning.

Vivian finished preparing the pot of soup then checked on Joshua. He slept. Shouldn't need feeding for a little while. "Do you mind watching the baby while I go outside?"

Mrs. Black looked up from working on her quilt. She'd made great progress. The frame had been rolled several times. She was almost at the center. "Go ahead. Me and the little one will be fine." Mrs. Black often asked to feed Joshua and spent hours rocking him or talking to him when he was awake.

It would soon enough be spring but a cold wind today denied the possibility. Vivian pulled on the borrowed coat and boots. She'd worn them so often she almost thought of them as hers. She slipped outside, closing the door as quickly as possible to keep out the cold and hurried, head down, to the barn. Billy had to have heard the squeal of the door and noticed the splash of light as she stepped inside, but he didn't look up from where he sat on a length of log surrounded by his cats and Limpy.

"Mind if I join you?"

"'Course not." He positioned another butt end of a log for her to sit on.

She sat and let half a dozen of the cats crowd around her, pulled the littlest to her lap, finding comfort and courage in cuddling it. "Billy, I don't like to think I have upset you."

"I been thinking."

"Come to any conclusions?" She ached for him to hold her and assure her everything would be fine, but she knew no matter what either of them decided, they would face problems. Life could not be easy like it was when she was a child.

"I thought you were happy here."

Her heart flipped over and lay like a frightened animal. She'd hoped for more than insistence that living here was all one needed. She prayed quickly before she answered him. *Lord, I need wisdom to make him understand that he needs to change as much as I do.* "I am happy here. But it isn't enough for the future."

"It's a fine place to live. I have the animals, a solid house—"

"Billy, this isn't about where you live. It's about how you live. I love the farm. I've found peace and contentment that I'd forgotten was possible. But I don't want to be a recluse. If I just had myself to think about it would be different but there's Joshua. And if we married, I hope there would be more children."

His face turned a glorious red then faded to white. "Children? You and me?"

She couldn't help but smile. "It usually happens to married folks. I wouldn't want them growing up afraid to see people. Would you?" Her words were very soft.

"No. But I wouldn't want them teased and tormented, either."

The argument was an endless circle. "I guess we

couldn't be guaranteed it wouldn't happen but there'd be those who welcomed them. Like the Morrows. Like your friend Lucas. Like Mr. Legal. There's probably a lot of people who would be friends if we give them a chance." He'd lived here so long, hidden from the public for his own sake as well as his mother's. How could she hope to persuade him it didn't have to continue? "Your ma is ready to move on."

"How can you know that?"

"She's taken many steps forward of late, hasn't she? Doesn't that indicate her readiness to change?"

"I gave up expecting any changes a long time ago."

She rested her hands over his fists. "I know you did. But it's time to try again."

"I don't know if I can."

"I think you can. If you want to."

He cupped his hand to the back of her head and pulled her forward to kiss her eyelids and her cheeks and finally, her mouth. She leaned into his kiss. She wanted this man as her husband to live together, to share their joys and sorrows. She said so to him.

"But not here?"

She grinned as she patted his chin. "Here is fine. I already said that. But not hiding. No more hiding."

"If you don't stay, where will you go?"

She jerked back, her heart crying silent tears that threatened to drown her. "You're saying no?"

"I don't know what I'm saying. But it seems to me you have no place else to go."

His words stung worse than she could imagine possible. "You think I have to stay by default. So you don't have to even try and change things?"

"I want it that way."

She jerked to her feet, scattering cats every direction. "Billy, it can't be that way. I won't let Joshua grow up afraid to face people. Thinking I don't want anyone to know about him because I'm ashamed of him."

Billy scrambled to his feet, too. "And I can't ask Ma to face the cruel things people say and do. She's content here. I can't take that from her."

The anger fled, leaving Vivian so weak she grabbed a post to steady herself. "Stop blaming your choice on your ma. It's because of your own fear of what people say that you won't go out in public unless you're forced to. It's time you stopped being afraid." She turned and stormed out.

She made it a few feet before she collapsed to the cold hard ground. *What was I thinking? That my love would be enough to change him. Give him the courage to face people.* How foolish she'd been. Again. Only this time, it hadn't been a sinful, shameful foolishness. It was an honorable, cherished thing that she would carry in a special place in her heart for the rest of her life.

Her heart heavy as field stone, she looked about at the low house, trees surrounding it, struggling for survival in a harsh land.

Here she'd found everything she'd longed for since she lost her parents. But now, it seemed she would be forced to choose between what her heart wanted and what she knew was best for her son. It was a far harsher choice than she could deal with. *God, help me do what is best.* She must move on. She must give Joshua the life he deserved. *If You see fit, help Billy to see that he can move on, too.* Yes, he protected his ma, she understood that and honored it, but he hid from his own fears, as well, whether he realized it or not.

She huddled over her knees and prayed for strength and wisdom, found comfort in recalling the scripture verses she'd heard from Billy's lips and from the mouth of Pastor Morrow. If only she had a Bible of her own to strengthen her soul in the days ahead—days she feared would be dark and difficult unless she kept her thoughts focused on God's Word.

Her limbs grew cold and she stiffly gained her feet and returned to the house, keeping her face turned away from Mrs. Black lest she see the depth of her pain and guess its source. She could not deal with questions and curiosity right now.

Billy plunked back down on the log end and let the cats crawl to his lap, his attention to them somewhat distracted.

Vivian loved him.

He nailed his heart and his hopes to that fact.

She felt she could conquer the world with her determination.

He knew she couldn't. Facing the people in church was only giving them more reason to whisper and gossip. And why would she want to do that? Create more for Joshua to endure?

Yet, his only defense was she had no place to go.

'Course she could find work somewhere, perhaps as a housekeeper or chambermaid in the hotel.

The very thought made him grind his teeth. He didn't want her in someone else's home. He wanted her in his.

He prayed fervently that no such opportunity would come her way.

She'd accused him of hiding because of his own fears of the public eye. It wasn't fear. It was unkind reality, which she would soon discover if she followed her plan. Nothing a person said or did could change the way people looked at him.

He would spare her the pain of discovering it for herself.

Dear God, look down on Vivian. Make a way to keep her here until she realizes how useless her plans are.

He returned to the house some time later but it wasn't the welcoming place he had grown content with. The air felt brittle as the argument they'd had crackled between them. He wanted to cradle her to his chest and assure her things would be fine. She just had to give herself time to sort them out. She soon announced lunch and he let the worries of the day slip away as he enjoyed the thick soup she'd made with bits of browned meat and a variety of vegetables.

A few days later, the midday sun slanted bright rays across the table. Full of warmth and the promise of spring, the bright light made Billy glad to be alive, especially with Vivian across the table from him and Joshua in her arms. She seemed so happy. So content. A Sunday had passed without her mentioning going to town. Perhaps she already reconsidered her plan.

Ma jerked to her feet, her eyes wide and filled with nervous fright. "Someone coming."

Billy blinked. He'd been so busy thinking how he enjoyed watching Vivian talk to the baby he hadn't even heard. "Sit down, Ma. I'll go see who it is." He strode outside to meet the rider. Mr. Legal.

His heart bounced against the soles of his boots. Did the man have news that would benefit or hurt Vivian?

Mr. Legal swung from his horse and rearranged his coattail before he thrust out a hand in greeting.

Billy shook it. "You've found out something?"

"I have. Is Miss Halliday still here?"

"Yup."

"Could I speak to her?"

Billy wanted to refuse. *Tell me. And I'll decide if I want you to tell her.* But it was Vivian's business. He had no right to interfere though his only concern was protecting her…and his own desire to keep her here, he reluctantly admitted. "Come along." He waved the man to the house.

Ma jerked from her chair as she saw the man with Billy and skittered headlong into her bedroom. Billy shot Vivian a pointed look. Did she really think Ma would ever be comfortable around strangers?

Mr. Legal didn't wait for an invite to sit but pulled out a chair and spread some papers. "I'm pleased to say you are the proud owner of your parents' home."

Vivian stared. "How can that be?"

"It seems your parents didn't owe more than a pittance at the bank. The proceeds of the auction were more than enough to pay off their debt."

"But Wayne said…" She stopped, her face flooding with guilty color.

"From what I can piece together, I think Wayne showed up at the Weimers' because he had business not with them, but with you. It would seem he went with the express purpose of getting you to sign papers giving the bank your house."

Vivian scrubbed her lips together and widened her eyes but not before Billy saw the glisten of tears. He knew she must be calling herself every kind of fool. He slipped to her side and squeezed her shoulder. She clung to his hand.

"I don't understand," she whispered.

"You were the sole heir and beneficiary of your parents' estate. The bank was to act as your agent until you were eighteen. They've been renting out the house and recently sold it. You're entitled to the rent monies."

She shuddered. "You said I owned the house. Didn't I foolishly sign it over to the bank?"

"The documents weren't witnessed legally. The Styleses realize their claim would not stand up in a court of law and have wisely backed away. The people who bought the house under false pretences are not legal owners."

"I'm sure they acted in good faith."

"Certainly, but they don't want to have anything to do with such dirty dealings so asked to have their money refunded. I think it would be only decent to do so. Now, let's get down to business. I need your signature here, here and here." He paused. "This time let's go over the documents and make sure you understand them." He explained the papers, paragraph by paragraph, and only when he was satisfied Vivian understood them did he allow her to sign.

A few minutes later he gathered up the documents and returned them to his brown leather carrying case. He shook Vivian's hand. "It's been a pleasure doing business with you. I should have the funds sorted out by Friday. Your house will be ready for you to move in around the same time."

Move in! The words blasted through Billy like a burning summer wind, drying up hope and blowing away his plans and dreams. Now she didn't have to stay. She could move into town and become part of normal life if anyone would let her. He spun around and stared out the window as his heart bounced around madly in his chest seeking a place to hitch its reins.

Vivian stared at the papers the lawyer had left her. She owned a house. Her childhood home. Her stomach reached for her backbone in a spasm of joy. She could hardly wait to see it.

Another thought grabbed the heels of her joy, dragging it bottomward.

She could move into town, begin a new life, face her past, build a future. The weight of the idea sucked at the skin on her face. She wanted things to be different. So much different. She wanted to share her future with Billy.

Billy had stayed at her side throughout the lawyer's visit, lending his support, but now he had moved away. Not just physically but mentally and emotionally.

She would make another appeal. Her strongest, most intense one. *Lord, please give me words that will convince him.* "Billy, I love you. You know I do. I love your home. You have made me so welcome. You have protected me and helped me. But my first concern must be what I think is best for Joshua. And now all of a sudden, I have a way of doing it."

"What if you're wrong?"

"What if you are? Billy, give people a chance. Give yourself a chance."

His ma came out of the room at that point, and

Vivian could say no more to try and convince Billy, but from the look on his face she knew she had failed to change his mind.

She could do no more than pray and leave it in God's hands, but the joy of getting her parents' home tasted dry and dusty as she faced following through on her choice.

Billy waited up for her as usual that evening. Their time alone contained a bittersweet element as she realized there would be so few of them. If only he would take a chance. They talked about everything but what really mattered as if he found it as painful as she.

She prayed fervently for things to change but Friday arrived and nothing had.

"You'll be wanting to head to town." Billy spoke with a sad note.

"The lawyer is expecting me." Her insides echoed his tone in increasing volume until she wanted to wrap her arms around herself and moan. How could they love each other and yet each be determined to go in separate directions? It just didn't seem right and yet she knew not how to change it. All the way to town she prayed for God to give them a way that would work for both of them.

But they drove up before the lawyer's office with no solution.

Billy remained in the wagon holding Joshua as Vivian went inside. She emerged a few minutes later feeling like she'd taken a step off the end of a walk and encountered nothing but thin air. Billy reached down to pull her to the seat. He sat considering her.

"You look as if a hard wind blew you off course."

"I've got money."

He chuckled. "Well, ain't that supposed to make a person happy?"

"I've never had more than a nickel in my pocket, ever." She now had a house and enough money to survive until she found a job or a position. This had to be God's way of assuring her she was doing the right thing. If only she didn't have to do it alone. But last night, Billy had reminded her of how his mother reacted to the lawyer's visit.

"Ma ain't ever going to be comfortable around strangers." His voice thickened.

She knew he ached over the impasse they had reached as much as she, which only intensified her pain until she wondered if she could contain it behind a smile and pleasant words. She pulled her thoughts back to her latest shock. "I have enough money to buy some nice things for Joshua. Maybe a toy." She could even make a new dress to replace the gray shapeless wonder provided by the Weimers. She should be excited. Instead, all she felt was a dull ache in the back of her head. She'd put off moving on as long as she could.

"Mr. Legal said I could go look at my house. It's empty."

"I'll take you."

She offered directions to the place. "There." She stared at the front door. There had once been a swing from that tree branch. And a special place beside the narrow veranda where she played with her dolls.

"Are you going in?"

She nodded and he jumped to the ground, Joshua still in one arm. She waited for Billy to assist her down and clung to his hand. "Come with me." Her insides quivered as she stared at her past with her future tucked against Billy's chest. It was an odd, disorienting feeling, like swinging too high and getting that little feeling of sailing onward free of the ropes just before the descending swing carried her backward.

"Come on. Let's have a look." The thickness of his voice was almost enough to make her change her mind and forget the whole business. But he headed up the path, pulling her along.

He thrust open the front door and stepped aside, giving her a chance to go in alone.

She took one tiny step and then another. The place was cold and empty except for a wing-backed chair with stuffing escaping the cushions, and an upturned bookshelf. The air still carried the smell of coal smoke and cinnamon. She stared straight ahead, mentally reviewing the rooms. Mother and Father's bedroom the first one on the left. Hers the second one. The kitchen through that door to the right with three more doors. One to a small storeroom, one to the guest bedroom and the third to the backyard where a big garden provided plenty of vegetables. Vivian had carried wash water out to the plants. Mother had also grown flowers along the front edge of the garden. "Beauty and practicality together," she always said. "Makes a good combination."

Most of all Vivian remembered how her parents had loved her. How her home had been a place of safety and warmth. She would provide the same for Joshua. She sucked in air until the quivering of her insides subsided.

"You going to look at anything else?"

Billy's voice jarred her into action. They explored the rooms. The former occupants had left behind a small table and two chairs in the kitchen. She found a chipped bowl in the cupboard. A bed frame had been left in the guest room and a dresser with a broken drawer in her bedroom.

"Not much to start over with," Billy said.

"I'll have to buy some supplies." She didn't need much in the way of furniture. "I'll fix the chair."

"You're determined to go through with this, are you?"

She faced him, her heart pressing hard against her ribs as she tried to be brave. "I have to do this." She touched Joshua's cheek. "For my son."

Billy caught Vivian's chin and tipped her face toward his. Their eyes met. At that moment, the sun dipped below the top of the window and poured golden light over them. Her insides felt kissed and blessed by the look of love in his eyes flashing back the glow of the sunshine. "Vivian, I love you." He bent his head and caught her mouth.

She leaned into him, drinking in his love. She wanted nothing more, nothing else, at least not for herself.

As if to remind her she must think of more than her own desires, Joshua kicked as if protesting being sandwiched between his mother and Billy.

She eased back, breaking the kiss with reluctance and only after two unsuccessful attempts. *Oh, Lord, how I love this man. There must be a way for us to be together.* "Billy, I love you so much I can't imagine not seeing your welcoming smile every morning across the table. But I have Joshua." She shuddered as the bright light of love faded from his eyes, replaced with a stormy sky of resignation.

"And I have Ma."

She wanted to beg him to forget his mother but if he would do so, he wasn't the man she loved. She wanted to tell him he could come and visit without his mother. But she knew his own fears were as strong as his ma's. "I can only pray that God will provide a way."

"In the meantime, you plan to move into this house?"

"Yes. As soon as possible. Tomorrow." She'd stay tonight but she wasn't prepared and she wanted just one more night at the farm, sharing the evening hours with Billy and seeing his smile over the breakfast table. She would etch those moments on her heart and carry them forever or until God saw fit to provide an answer for them.

They made the trip back home in relative quiet as if neither of them could think beyond what the morrow held.

And that night, as they shared their customary evening hours, Billy shifted the conversation to his past.

"Pa used to take me to church."

"Did he have a strong faith?" Suddenly, it seemed she must know everything about Billy from the time he was a baby. She might not get a chance to ask him later.

"Pa said, 'A man takes what God gives him and tries to make the best of it.' I guess I've tried to do the same."

Vivian knew he meant taking care of his mother. "My mother said it's darkest just before the dawn."

At the meaning of the words, their gazes locked. Could dawn be approaching for them? She didn't see how. She'd gone so far as to suggest to Mrs. Black that things might be different now if she were to go to town. Perhaps she'd find she could be part of normal life. The woman had scrubbed her hair into wild disarray and dashed outside, pausing only long enough to grab her coat. Perhaps Mrs. Black had lived this way too long, couldn't change now.

She blinked, pulling back the pain that crawled up

and down her insides, dragging cruel nails in its fist. "Tell me about your pa."

He shifted as Joshua fussed, and hummed until the baby settled again. "Pa seemed to shrink after Ma came back." He chuckled softly, mindful of the content baby on his chest. "I just realized it wasn't Pa who shrank but me who grew way bigger than him. He was a good man, patient, unruffled by…" He stopped as if surprised by his thoughts.

"Yes?"

"He never let what people say bother him. Said they only spoke out of their own fears or ignorance and we wouldn't act any differently if the shoe was on the other foot."

Thank You, Lord. You are at work. Wisely, she didn't choose to comment on Billy's observation, certain he would realize the importance of what he'd said without her help.

He continued to talk about his father until they retired to bed.

Chapter Fifteen

If Vivian thought her prayers had been answered, her hopes were flattened the next morning. Billy carried items from the room where he'd been sleeping—a small rocker he fixed a broken rung on, a battered pot and some dishes. "If you're going to live in town you'll need more than a bed. Good thing Ma keeps everything."

Vivian kept her disappointment stuffed in the pit of her stomach as she prepared breakfast and Billy continued to haul things out to the wagon. He soon had a fair-sized load. "I can't take all that stuff."

"Nothing we've any use for, ain't that right, Ma?"

Mrs. Black watched Billy make the trips back and forth, her expression growing more and more troubled. "You're leaving?"

"I told you, Ma. She got her parents' house back. She's going to live in town."

"You'll be taking Joshua?" The woman's voice quivered.

"You can come visit anytime." Vivian watched carefully, hoping to see a hint of agreement.

Instead, Mrs. Black windmilled her arms. "I don't go to town. Never go to town. Never."

Vivian pressed her lips together to still the cry of disappointment. She met Billy's gaze and saw his resignation and remembered his words of last night. *Try and make the best of things.*

She didn't want him to accept this way of life. She turned away so he couldn't see the depth of her pain. There was nothing he could do to change things. She had to accept that. But the bottom of her heart threatened to push clear up her throat and choke her.

They ate in silence. Vivian didn't know what either of the Blacks felt but she felt like she ate the condemned man's last meal.

She and Billy did dishes together, sadness making her limbs heavy. Mrs. Black huddled over her quilt now almost finished. She'd removed it from the frame a few days ago to begin stitching the edging on.

Vivian loved the design and wished she could see the quilt completed. But watching Mrs. Black working feverishly as if each jab of the needle could poke holes in the tense atmosphere filled her with such a long, dark ache she wanted to cry. Why couldn't the woman change? Just a little. Just enough to set Billy free.

Vivian was almost grateful when they finished the dishes and scurried to gather up the last of her things. She wrapped Joshua against the cool air and paused. "Goodbye, Mrs. Black. Thank you for allowing me to stay. And if you ever get the notion to visit me, I'd be pleased to see you."

She waited. Mrs. Black didn't even look up. "Goodbye."

Just as she stepped out the door, Mrs. Black called, "Wait." She bundled up the quilt and rushed to Vivian's side. "It's yours. Take it." She pushed the quilt into Vivian's arms.

The woman had been in a hurry to finish so she could gift Vivian with the quilt. Vivian was so surprised she couldn't speak. She swallowed hard, forced words to her wooden tongue. "Thank you. I will cherish it always."

"Well, I'll be," Billy murmured, as he helped Vivian into the wagon.

Vivian didn't speak all the way to town. She couldn't. She was too busy trying to control emotions that raced through an endless circle of surprise, sadness, determination and hope. Hope that this gift was a sign Mrs. Black was changing. As quickly as she thought it might be possible, her doubts and sadness returned. Giving a gift was a far cry from changing how she lived.

They arrived at her house and Billy quickly unloaded the things he'd brought. He carried in a feather tick and slapped it into shape on the bed frame he'd moved into her former room.

Too soon, the wagon stood empty.

Vivian tried unsuccessfully to still the panic pressing against her heart. Soon she'd be alone, facing her future. Joshua lay in the little bed Billy had made. She stared at her son. For him. She was doing all this for him, but at her side Billy stood, his hands stuffed in his pockets.

"I guess I better be on my way. Leave you to get settled."

She turned slowly, her limbs rubbery. She managed a strangled whisper. "Stay. I'll make supper."

Regret wreathed his face, making his blue eyes cloudy. "Vivian, I can't. You don't want people to start talk, now, do you?"

She shook her head, although at this very moment she didn't care what cruel things the neighbors might think or say. But look where not caring had gotten her.

"'Sides, Ma will be 'specting me." He made no move toward the door.

Vivian's face felt as if the skin might sag off the bones. Her chest, on the other hand, had turned stiff except for a spot in her chest where all the pain of this parting burrowed deep, with agonizing insistence.

"I don't want you to go."

Billy groaned. "Then come back with me. Marry me and live on the farm."

From somewhere inside, an indisputable argument

forced its way into her thoughts. She loved the farm. Would gladly live there but she wouldn't hide. Especially not hide Joshua. "When life at the farm can be normal."

"Vivian, it won't happen. Not while Ma's alive."

She nodded. They both knew it. They both had to live with the fact. But oh, how it hurt to say goodbye. She searched his face, memorizing every dear, familiar detail. She pressed trembling fingers to his cheeks. "You will visit me, won't you?"

He shook his head. "It wouldn't be appropriate." His words caught. He closed his eyes and turned his face to kiss the palm of her hand. Then he caught her to him and held her securely against his big chest.

She wanted to beg him to change for her sake. Somehow, they could work this out. He could protect his mother and still live a normal life if he would only…

What? What did she expect he would do? He felt this was the only way he could make up for hiding when his ma was captured—sharing a life that put no expectations on her. She understood. But she wished it could be different.

"You must do what you must do for Joshua and I must take care of Ma."

"You're right. Tomorrow, I will go to church and confront the congregation. I will start over with God's forgiveness and whatever forgiveness people choose to extend to me."

"And I will take care of Ma."

She clutched his shirtfront and breathed in his warm familiar scent. "If only things could be different." She had only one hope. "I pray something will change."

He cupped a big, protective hand to her neck. A shudder shook him. "Since I became a man, all I've wanted was a wife and family. Then I accepted I could never have it. Not with Ma the way she is about seeing people. And then you and Josh came into my life." He tipped her head back so he could examine her eyes, her hair, her chin.

The hunger in his eyes filled her with an ache as deep as a canyon, as wide as the Dakota sky and as dry as the winds that blew across the prairie.

Billy continued. "I will cherish each moment I have spent with you. I will see your face in every sunset. I will hear your laugh in the wind through the treetops. I will see your smile each time Limpy greets me. I will pray for you every day and fall asleep with your name on my lips. And I will miss you with every beat of my heart."

Vivian quivered with emotion. Never had she heard Billy so eloquent. His words were sweet as dew on the petals of a rose and as painful as the thorns on the same bush. She didn't realize she cried until he thumbed the tears from her cheeks.

He bent and tenderly claimed her mouth, his kiss lingering.

Greedily, she returned his kiss, wanting to weld him there forever.

He broke away and with long strides headed for the door. He paused, turned. "Vivian, I love you."

"I love you, too." More than he could know. More than she thought possible. She'd never felt anything as powerful as this before.

But he left in such a hurry she didn't know if he even heard.

Billy couldn't remember the trip home. He couldn't remember putting Blaze in his stall. He ate the food Ma set before him without tasting it and he must have washed the dishes because the kitchen was tidy. He sat in his big chair before the fire and stared at the flames without seeing them.

He'd been content enough before Vivian blew into his life on the tail of a storm. But he would never know that contentment again. Every corner of the house echoed with memories of her and the baby. Every breath he drew vibrated with his loneliness. How he'd endure he did not know. He only knew he must somehow convince Ma it didn't matter.

"Is Vivian's house nice?"

Ma's question startled him. He'd almost forgotten she sat in the chair across from him, carding wool for her next quilt.

"Pretty little house." He didn't have to close his eyes to see Vivian hurrying about, putting things away, adjusting the position of each piece of furniture until she was satisfied. He crossed his arms over his chest to still the hunger for her.

"She'll be happy there?"

Why did it matter to Ma? No doubt she was glad to have the woman and child out of her home. Billy sucked in air until he coughed. No need for him to blame Ma for things beyond her control.

Missing Vivian was a pain so real, so demanding, he had to chance upsetting Ma. "Ma, do you think you might like to go to town in the future?"

He waited, hoping, praying.

She stopped rocking. "I ain't been to town since…" She shook her head. "I can't."

He knew her answer before she gave it. Yet unless she changed—

She rocked furiously, her eyes wide with fright.

His hopes wilted. She could not change and he would never walk away from her. He'd been powerless at six to defend her, protect her. He wasn't now.

He flipped open a newspaper but the words made no sense. He couldn't stop thinking about Vivian. If only it was possible for them to enjoy their love.

He rattled the pages and forced himself to continue reading. Ma was not an obstacle. She was his glad responsibility. She must never guess at how much it cost him to give up Vivian. He did not want to make her feel bad for something she couldn't help—her fear of people and of change.

Why had God sent Vivian into his life? Was it meant for good? *It's time to start new.* That's what Vivian said.

But Ma would not change. He didn't want to upset her. He'd long ago learned to do so meant sending her into one of her spells.

Loving Vivian had changed things for him but unless Ma changed, he must endure this pain until it somehow developed a scab. Even then it would fester. Forever.

Could he trust God to change Ma so their love was possible?

He bowed his head and prayed for a long time, confessing that he hadn't trusted God nor asked His help. *Lord, let Ma be willing to change.* If she wasn't, he must be ready to let this whole business rest in God's hands. No longer did he feel so powerless. Surely, God would work things out.

"Ma, we've hidden long enough. I want to start living again. A new life." He sucked in air. If she knew how important it was and why— "Ma, I love Vivian. But I can't expect her to hide here like we do."

Ma stopped rocking. Only her hands continued the restless motion. Her gaze darted to the fire, remained there a moment then slowly came to him.

He saw the dark fear in her eyes. His conscience smote him. How could he torment his ma like this? "Ma, I won't go. I'll always be here for you."

She nodded. "I'm sorry. I'm sorry. I'm sorry."

He caught her hands. "Ma, stop. It's fine."

She held his gaze in an endless search.

He wished he could read her thoughts and guess what went through her mind as she studied him.

She picked up her project and resumed the soothing routine of combing the wool.

That should have been the end of it for him. He would not upset Ma anymore. But he lay again in his own bed where Vivian had slept these past weeks, every breath full of her scent, every inch of skin missing her, he could not stop wishing and dreaming, missing and aching.

He didn't sleep much. He prayed. He thought of Vivian and Joshua in town. He thought of Vivian standing before the congregation in the morning.

And he made up his mind.

He told Ma at breakfast. "I'm going to church."

She dropped her knife. "Church?"

"Yes, Ma. Vivian is planning to publicly confess her sin before the whole congregation. I can't let her do that by herself. I will be there to stand at her side."

Ma kept her head down as if his announcement signaled his departure forever.

"Ma, I'll be back but I can't let her face this alone."

"I did some serious thinking last night." She faced him, her eyes wide, her lips trembling. Something flickered through her eyes. "I've kept you here long enough. I've hidden long enough." Her voice hardened with determination. "I'll go to church with you." She shivered.

"Ma, that's great."

"Maybe only this once. Depends."

It was a start. God willing, it would be more than that.

They hurried through chores and donned their best clothes. He eyed Ma. "You might enjoy going to town and picking out fabric for a new dress."

"Billy, I'm not promising anything but this one time. Besides—" she smoothed her hands over her skirt "—I quite like the fabric you pick out."

A few minutes later they sat side by side on the wagon seat and headed for town. Billy had been so many times in the last few weeks that it was almost commonplace, but this time he would confront a crowd of people, many who had been cruel in the past.

Ma's anxiety pulsated along her arm and up his until his nerves vibrated.

Only one thing kept him going—the thought of Vivian standing at the front, alone and vulnerable.

The service had started by the time they arrived.

He hesitated, sucked in air. "Let's go, Ma."

She clutched his hand. "I can't. You go ahead."

Aah. Pain caught him just below his ribs and knuckled deep and hard. He'd hoped this was the beginning. He'd hoped this meant he could dream of a future with Vivian. It took all his strength to push back his disappointment. "Ma, I must go in."

"I'll wait here."

He didn't have time to argue. He didn't want to miss being with Vivian.

He jogged to the door and paused, remembering. Now was not the time to think of the way he'd been laughed at in the past. He closed his mind to such things and slipped in as quietly as he could to stand in the entryway where he had a good view of the front of the church.

Vivian stood before the congregation, holding Joshua proudly in her arms. It was so quiet. Was he too late? He stood, his hat in his hands, trying to decide what to do.

Vivian smiled. "Thank you for the chance to speak to all of you. This is my son, Joshua. Now I could pretend I am a widow and that would it make too easy for all of us. But I'm not. What you see before you is a woman who has sinned. I confess to my shame and sorrow. Except I am not ashamed or sorry to have this precious child. He is a treasure and it is for him that I am willing to face you and make this confession. Yes, I have sinned. For a time, I thought I must live condemned and guilty, but Pastor Morrow showed me many verses that prove God's love and forgiveness for even one like me. One verse I will cling to is First John, chapter one, verse nine. 'If we confess our sin, he is faithful and just to forgive us our sins, and to cleanse us from all unrighteousness.' I don't deserve His mercy and forgiveness but I won't refuse it, either.

"I'm very glad to be back in the town where I spent my happy childhood. I look around and recognize some of you. I remember how good and kind you were to me in the past.

"God has forgiven me and I pray you can find it in your heart to forgive me, too. And if you don't, well, I don't blame you."

Billy thought he would burst with pride at her strength and confidence.

She drew in a shaky breath and adjusted Joshua. "For Joshua's sake, I ask you not to blame him for what I've done. But whatever each of you decides, I am going to live here even if I have to walk alone."

Billy pushed into the sanctuary. She would not be walking alone. Ignoring the startled whispers, he strode to the front of the church and went to her side.

Her smile was trembling, her eyes grateful.

"I'm here." He didn't know what else to say. He wanted to promise her he would walk boldly at her side always but a great gulf of fears held him back. Ma's fears only, he realized. He no longer cared what people said or did. But he still must provide Ma with the security she needed. He owed her that much.

A surprised ripple had people turning to the back of the church.

Both he and Vivian gasped. Ma stood, arm in arm with Mrs. Morrow. Ma caught his eyes and nodded. He knew exactly what she meant.

She and Mrs. Morrow sat in a pew close to the back.

The congregation settled and faced forward again, all eyes on Billy and Vivian.

He knew they expected something more and, with a wide grin, he prepared to give it to them. "Vivian, you will not have to walk through town on your own. I'll be at your side each step of the way. If you will have me, I will be your husband and Joshua's father."

"I will have you," she whispered.

Billy drank in her eager smile, then faced the congregation. "It is time for a new start."

He noted some of the elderly ladies dabbing hankies to their eyes.

Pastor Morrow stood at the pulpit. "Billy is right. But I doubt that Vivian and Billy or Mrs. Black are the only ones who need to put things right or find a way to start over. Whether it's with friends or family or with God, why not do it today?"

Billy and Vivian sat in the front pew as the pastor spoke.

"Let us pray." The pastor prayed for forgiveness, honesty and humility and for those who needed cleansing to have the boldness to seek it. When he finished, more than a dozen people made their way to the front and knelt at the steps.

A holy hush filled the place until the organist played, then people quietly departed, leaving behind those who wanted to pray.

People gathered in the yard. Many went to Ma and shook her hand. She looked more stunned than afraid.

Billy hoped because she found the welcome over-whelming.

He stood, his arm around Vivian. A continual parade of people came to congratulate them. Some shied away, averting their eyes. Billy knew not everyone would welcome them. He didn't expect it. In fact, this was more than he'd thought possible.

"Come to my house for lunch."

"Ma?"

"Her, too. It makes it respectable, after all." Her eyes twinkled and he laughed.

They slipped away. After they ate, Ma offered to feed little Josh.

"Come for a walk?" Billy said.

She nodded and grabbed her cape.

Spring was in the air and they walked away from town, enjoying the sound of returning songbirds and the warm breeze. She tucked her arm around his and snuggled close. "I love you, Big Billy Black."

The nickname that had once made him feel like a monster sounded like a trophy on her lips and he laughed loud and hard, not caring if people would hear him and wonder.

He waited until they reached the edge of town and found the shelter of a budding tree to pull her into his arms. "I love you, Vivian Halliday. My love, my dream, my everything. When can we get married?"

Vivian's laugh was silenced by his kiss.

Epilogue

Vivian held the squirming Joshua in her arms as they waited for Billy. At the sound of the approaching wagon, Josh kicked and babbled with excitement and leaned toward the door, his arms extended for the greeting he knew he would get. "Hang on, Daddy will be here in a minute."

Thank you, Lord, for the love of this good man and for the love he has for my son.

They married that spring and had enjoyed six months of wedded joy in a summer as warm and wonderful as their love.

Billy burst through the door. "You ready?" He kissed Vivian on the nose and Josh on the top of his head.

Vivian laughed. "You're almost as excited as I am."

He took Josh and shepherded her out the door. He offered his hand to help her up, then kissed Josh before he put the baby on her lap. "I'm excited just to be alive." The wagon creaked as he climbed up to sit beside her. "I can't believe how wonderful life is." He slipped his arms around her and kissed her thoroughly before he took up the reins. "Blessed, I am."

She tucked her hand around his arm and nuzzled her cheek on his thick solid arm. "Me, too, my sweet man. Me, too."

It seemed only moments before they arrived in town. Several people looked up as they passed and waved. Vivian squeezed Billy's arm. People had been so good to them. Not everyone, of course, but it grew easier and easier to ignore those who turned away.

She still regretted that Wayne had turned his back on his son but it was a relief when the Styleses had moved. She didn't know how many people knew of their shady dealings with her and she'd never tell. In fact, she would do all she could to protect Joshua from being identified with his biological father. Someday, when he was older, if he wanted to know she might tell him all the sordid details, but for now…

"Want to leave Joshua with his gramma while we tend to business?"

"She'd have our hide if we didn't."

They looked into each other's eyes, openly, silently loving each other and sharing their amazement and joy at how far his ma had come from the frightened, strange lady of the past.

"Vivian, I can now readily admit what I once denied, that I was hiding for my sake as much as for Ma's."

She understood more than he knew. "And now?"

"I'm proud to walk openly because people see how much you love me. I never want to hide that from people."

Her throat tightened at the way he looked at her all proud and grateful. He turned the wagon down the side street toward Vivian's house where his mother now lived. She had a circle of friends who were as avid about quilting as she. Her interests had grown to knitting. She and her friends had a passion to supply quilts and knit goods to those less fortunate. Vivian's heart drank in sweet delight at their latest project. A woman in their group had opened her house to a family of three children left orphaned. She vowed to keep them together and give them love and nurturing. Ma Black and her friends promised to help in every way they could. Some of the money the bank had given back to Vivian had helped purchase goods for the newly formed family.

They left Josh in the loving arms of his grandmother and turned down the street toward the church where Billy stopped the wagon and helped Vivian to the ground.

She clung to his hand as she crossed the yellowed grass. With a start, she realized fall was upon them already. Then she forgot everything but what she had come to see.

A simple stone marker she'd purchased with some of her windfall money.

Two names were carved into it.

Joshua Halliday. His birth date, the date of his death. Isabelle Morton Halliday. The dates of her birth and death. And a verse Vivian had chosen. "Nothing shall be able to separate us from the love of God, which is in Christ Jesus our Lord."

She knelt on the ground before the graves and bowed her head.

Billy cupped his hand across the back of her neck.

Momma, Poppa. I made so many mistakes. Some so big. But not even that can keep me from God's love. I will see you some glad day in glory. Until then, goodbye. I love you.

She scrubbed tears from her cheeks. She would miss them always. But she had a new family—a husband, a son and a mother-in-law who had observed much and thought deeply during her years of isolation and now seemed an endless fount of wisdom and keen wit. Perhaps, God willing, there would be more children. How her parents would have loved to see her grown and with a child.

And she had a husband who grew more dear with each passing moment. She pushed to her feet and turned into his arms. "I love you, Billy Black."

He kissed her soundly and tucked her against his chest as they returned to the wagon. "I have one more stop to make before we go home."

They drove straight down the main street toward the store. "Wait here." He strode in the front door as bold and at ease as if he'd done it all his life.

He returned almost at once, carrying a large package. Lucas, at his side, carried a smaller one.

Curious, she demanded, "What do you have?"

"Something for my sweet wife. But you have to wait until we get home."

"Not fair." They had to stop and visit his ma and then there was the ride home. "I can't wait that long."

"You don't have much choice."

"I could climb in the back and unwrap it right here."

His eyes twinkled. "Think you can outwrestle me?"

She giggled at the absurdity, then crossed her arms and faced straight ahead, determined she wouldn't let him know she was dying of curiosity.

But by the time they reached home she had practically crawled out of her skin.

And Billy knew it. He took his time about carrying Josh inside and sitting him on the floor to play with a soft ball his grandma had knit for him.

"Now?" she asked.

"You sit, and I'll bring it in."

She sat and folded her hands.

Satisfied, he returned to the wagon. First, he brought in the bigger parcel and set it on the stool. She scrambled to tear off the brown paper.

She gasped when she saw what it was. Her throat closed off with a rush of emotions. "Blue Boy. Where did you get this?"

"Lift it up."

She did so. "Pinky." Tears flowed like a river. She shook her head and choked out, "How?"

"You spoke of them so often I had to see if I could track them down. I found the auctioneer who had sold your parents' things and he kindly gave me the name of the people who bought the pictures. The people gladly sold them back when I explained why I wanted them."

"Thank you." She tipped her face upward, inviting a kiss and was rewarded with a gentle one.

"Where will we hang them?" She glanced around, choosing a place.

"Don't you want to see the other parcel?"

She'd forgotten it. "I can't imagine anything better than this."

"I could take it back, I suppose."

"No, you don't. Bring it in."

He placed the parcel in her lap. Some solid object. She folded back the papers to reveal a Bible. She opened the flyleaf and read the family registry of her parents and their wedding and her own birth. "It's my parents' Bible." She stroked the cover, ran her finger over the names and felt a cord of belonging in her connection to these names. "I can't believe you found this."

"It is rightfully yours. Now you can add our marriage and Joshua's birth to the family history."

She hugged the Bible to her chest. "It feels like I have come full circle from the love of my parents to the love of a good man."

"Full circle. I like that." He knelt before her and

wrapped her in his warm love. "And we build another circle on top of that."

Their love would go on and on—a circle of endless love.

* * * * *

We hope you enjoyed DAKOTA CHILD by bestselling author Linda Ford. Share this book with friends and give the gift of romance to others. See page 277 to find some ideas for sharing your books, and make someone feel as special as you do.

Look for Linda Ford's upcoming titles from Love Inspired Historical!

CHRISTMAS UNDER WESTERN SKIES
(with Anna Schmidt)
"A COWBOY'S CHRISTMAS"
December 2010

DAKOTA FATHER
January 2011

PRAIRIE COWBOY
March 2011

KLONDIKE MEDICINE WOMAN
May 2011
ALASKAN BRIDES

Dear Reader,

When I started this story I was interested in exploring how loving a child gives people an incentive to make tremendous changes in their lives. I'm sure we've all experienced this to some degree, even if we aren't parents. Children, especially babies, are so helpless that it brings out protectiveness in us, and in many cases drives us to take steps that we wouldn't have had the strength to do before or perhaps haven't even seen the need of. As it turned out, the characters in my story had lots to overcome and loving a tiny baby did, indeed, prove to help them on their journey, as did their love for each other.

I hope, as you go along with Billy and Vivian on their journey, you will be encouraged in your own faith walk.

I love to hear from readers. Contact me through e-mail at linda@lindaford.org. Feel free to check on updates and bits about my research at my Web site, www. lindaford. org.

God bless,

Linda Ford

QUESTIONS FOR DISCUSSION

1. When Billy was young, his family was attacked by Indians. How did this attack affect their lives? Is it still affecting them now?

2. When Vivian's parents died of a fever, leaving her an orphan, she was sent to an orphanage by the town elders. What could they have done instead?

3. Billy believes people see his size as a reason to mistrust him. What could he have done to prove them wrong?

4. What drove Vivian to get pregnant out of wedlock? What did she learn about herself through that? Is there some way she could have found what she needed some other way?

5. Vivian believes she can make everything all right by finding Joshua's father. Do you agree with her plan? Why or why not?

6. Billy remembers Vivian showing him kindness when they were younger. Why did that make such an impression on him and what does it reveal about Vivian?

7. While Vivian stays at Billy's house, she is some-what afraid of Billy and his mother. Does she have good reason? Does she handle it well or could you suggest other ways for her to deal with having to stay with this pair?

8. At what point in the story did you know Vivian had faced her pain and was ready to start over as a responsible adult?

9. At what point did you know for certain that Billy had conquered his past?

10. Vivian knows she did wrong in engaging in sex outside marriage. Pastor Morrow reminds her that none of us is without sin. How is she prepared to deal with her sin?

11. Billy cannot, in good conscience, abandon his mother. Would you have done the same in his place? Why or why not?

12. All his life Billy has longed for the very things Vivian offers him—home, family and love. Yet he struggles to accept them. What is it that finally enables him to move past his fear of people's words?

13. Do you foresee a happy future for this couple? What lessons do they learn that will strengthen them in whatever challenges they face?

*Enjoy a sneak peek at Valerie Hansen's adventurous
historical-romance novel RESCUING THE HEIRESS,
available February, only from Love Inspired Historical*

"I think your profession is most honorable."

One more quick glance showed him that Tess was smiling, and it was all he could do to keep from breaking into a face-splitting grin at her praise. There was something impish yet charming about the banker's daughter. Always had been, if he were totally honest with himself.

Someday, Michael vowed silently, he would find a suitable woman with a spirit like Tess's and give her a proper courting. He had no chance with Tess herself, of course. That went without saying. Still, she couldn't be the only appealing lass in San Francisco. Besides, most men waited to wed until they could properly look after a wife and family.

If he'd been a rich man's son instead of the offspring of a lowly sailor, however, perhaps he'd have shown a personal interest in Miss Clark or one of her socialite friends already.

Would he really have? he asked himself. He doubted it. There was a part of Michael that was repelled by the affectations of the wealthy, by the way they lorded it over the likes of him and his widowed mother. He knew Tess couldn't help that she'd been born into a life of luxury, yet he still found her background off-putting.

Which is just as well, he reminded himself. It was bad enough that they were likely to be seen out and about on this particular evening. If the maid Annie Dugan hadn't been along as a chaperone, he knew their time together could, if misinterpreted, lead to his ruination. His career with the fire department depended upon a sterling reputation as well as a

Spartan lifestyle and strong work ethic.

Michael had labored too long and hard to let anything spoil his pending promotion to captain. He set his jaw and grasped the reins of the carriage more tightly. Not even the prettiest, smartest, most persuasive girl in San Francisco was going to get away with doing that.

He sighed, realizing that Miss Tess Clark fit that description to a T.

You won't be able to put down the rest of
Tess and Michael's romantic love story,
available in February 2011,
only from Love Inspired Historical.

Spread the joy of love and romance!

Dakota Child is a heartwarming story about a single mom who gets lost in a terrible Dakota winter storm, and the man who opens up his home and his heart to her, while trying to overcome his own hardships. This is a story you can share with friends, family, book club members or anyone you think would enjoy an inspirational, romantic read!

Here are some ideas for sharing books:

◆ Give to your sister, daughter, granddaughter, mother, friends or coworkers
◆ Host your own book club
◆ Share the books with members of your church group, community group or PTA
◆ Share them at your community center, retirement home or hospital and brighten someone's day

OR

◆ Leave them for others to enjoy on an airplane, in a coffee shop, at the Laundromat, doctor's/dentist's office, hairdresser, spa or vacation spot

Please tell us about your experience reading and sharing these books at

www.tellharlequin.com.

Love Inspired
HISTORICAL
INSPIRATIONAL HISTORICAL ROMANCE

Save $1.00 on the purchase of
Rescuing the Heiress by
Valerie Hansen or any other
Love Inspired® Historical title.

On Sale
February 8

SAVE
$1.⁰⁰

on the purchase of *Rescuing the Heiress*
by Valerie Hansen or any other
Love Inspired® Historical title.

Coupon expires June 30, 2011. Redeemable at participating retail outlets
in the U.S. and Canada only. Limit one coupon per customer.

52609624

Canadian Retailers: Harlequin Enterprises Limited will pay the face value
of this coupon plus 10.25¢ if submitted by customer for this product only. Any
other use constitutes fraud. Coupon is nonassignable. Void if taxed, prohibited
or restricted by law. Consumer must pay any government taxes. Void if copied.
Nielsen Clearing House ("NCH") customers submit coupons and proof of sales to
Harlequin Enterprises Limited, P.O. Box 3000, Saint John, NB E2L 4L3, Canada.
Non-NCH retailer—for reimbursement submit coupons and proof of sales directly
to Harlequin Enterprises Limited, Retail Marketing Department, 225 Duncan Mill
Rd., Don Mills, ON M3B 3K9, Canada.

5 65373 00076 2   (8100)0 11720

U.S. Retailers: Harlequin Enterprises
Limited will pay the face value of this coupon
plus 8¢ if submitted by customer for this
product only. Any other use constitutes fraud.
Coupon is nonassignable. Void if taxed,
prohibited or restricted by law. Consumer must
pay any government taxes. Void if copied. For
reimbursement submit coupons and proof of
sales directly to Harlequin Enterprises Limited,
P.O. Box 880478, El Paso, TX 88588-0478,
U.S.A. Cash value 1/100 cents.

LIHBAPCOUP

REQUEST YOUR FREE BOOKS!

2 FREE INSPIRATIONAL NOVELS
PLUS 2
FREE
MYSTERY GIFTS

Love Inspired

HISTORICAL
INSPIRATIONAL HISTORICAL ROMANCE

YES! Please send me 2 FREE Love Inspired® Historical novels and my 2 FREE mystery gifts (gifts are worth about $10). After receiving them, if I don't wish to receive any more books, I can return the shipping statement marked "cancel". If I don't cancel, I will receive 4 brand-new novels every other month and be billed just $4.24 per book in the U.S. or $4.74 per book in Canada. That's a saving of over 20% off the cover price. It's quite a bargain! Shipping and handling is just 50¢ per book.* I understand that accepting the 2 free books and gifts places me under no obligation to buy anything. I can always return a shipment and cancel at any time. Even if I never buy another book, the two free books and gifts are mine to keep forever.

102/302 IDN E7QD

Name _____ (PLEASE PRINT) _____

Address _____ Apt. #

City _____ State/Prov. _____ Zip/Postal Code

Signature (if under 18, a parent or guardian must sign)

Mail to **Steeple Hill Reader Service:**
IN U.S.A.: P.O. Box 1867, Buffalo, NY 14240-1867
IN CANADA: P.O. Box 609, Fort Erie, Ontario L2A 5X3
Not valid for current subscribers to Love Inspired Historical books.

Want to try two free books from another series?
Call 1-800-873-8635 or visit www.morefreebooks.com.

* Terms and prices subject to change without notice. Prices do not include applicable taxes. Sales tax applicable in N.Y. Canadian residents will be charged applicable provincial taxes and GST. Offer not valid in Quebec. This offer is limited to one order per household. All orders subject to approval. Credit or debit balances in a customer's account(s) may be offset by any other outstanding balance owed by or to the customer. Please allow 4 to 6 weeks for delivery. Offer available while quantities last.

Your Privacy: Steeple Hill Books is committed to protecting your privacy. Our Privacy Policy is available online at www.SteepleHill.com or upon request from the Reader Service. From time to time we make our lists of customers available to reputable third parties who may have a product or service of interest to you. If you would prefer we not share your name and address, please check here. ☐

Help us get it right—We strive for accurate, respectful and relevant communications. To clarify or modify your communication preferences, visit us at www.ReaderService.com/consumerchoice.

LIH10R

HARLEQUIN®

A *Romance*

FOR EVERY MOOD™

Experience the variety
of romances that
Harlequin has to offer...

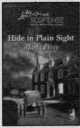